HIS TO
PROTECT

RED STONE SECURITY SERIES

Katie Reus

Cover art: Jaycee of Sweet 'N Spicy Designs
Author website: http://www.katiereus.com

His to Protect/Katie Reus. -- 1st ed.
ISBN-13: 978-1497447233
ISBN-10: 1497447232

eISBN: 9780988617131

*For my mom, who taught me
how to be a mother by example.*

Praise for the novels of Katie Reus

"Sinful, Sexy, Suspense... Katie Reus pulls you in and never lets go."
—*New York Times* bestselling author, Laura Wright

"Has all the right ingredients: a hot couple, evil villains, and a killer action-filled plot. . . . [The] Moon Shifter series is what I call Grade-A entertainment!" —Joyfully Reviewed

"I could not put this book down. . . . Let me be clear that I am not saying that this was a good book *for* a paranormal genre; it was an excellent romance read, *period.*" —All About Romance

"Reus strikes just the right balance of steamy sexual tension and nail-biting action....This romantic thriller reliably hits every note that fans of the genre will expect." —*Publishers Weekly*

"Explosive danger and enough sexual tension to set the pages on fire . . . fabulous!" —*New York Times* bestselling author, Alexandra Ivy

"Nonstop action, a solid plot, good pacing and riveting suspense..."
—*RT Book Reviews (4.5 Stars)*

CHAPTER ONE

"That is one hell of an ass," Vincent murmured to Kell.

Following the other man's gaze, Kell grunted the expected agreement, then froze. That *was* a nice ass. The best he'd ever seen. He'd also held onto it as the woman it belonged to wrapped her legs around him while he pumped into her for hours.

Though Charlotte's back was to him, the formfitting red dress clung to her sleek—and a little curvier than he remembered—body like a second skin. In an opulent room where most of the men and women were wearing black or other dark formalwear, she stood out like a beacon. It wasn't intentional, either. Even if she'd been wearing simple black, she'd have shined as brightly. The woman just seemed to glow. With dark hair, smooth pale skin, lush lips and an elegant bearing, she was the kind of woman men wrote fucking poems about. Well, not men like him, but she certainly inspired that kind of shit.

Right now her dark hair was piled on her head in some sort of complicated twist, revealing just how deep the V of that dress went. She wasn't showing too much skin exactly, but he didn't like the thought of other men seeing her. He nearly snorted. It wasn't like he had a claim on her. Hell, he hadn't even seen her in a year. Still…his gaze trailed over all that smooth skin and all he could picture was how she'd looked bent over her bed as he'd trailed kisses along her spine and backside.

He straightened, placing the still-full champagne flute he'd never intended to drink in the first place on the tray of a passing server. As part of their security cover tonight, he, Vincent and another dozen men and women were posing as guests at the extravagant party. The couple having the party didn't want overt security. Didn't want to offend their wealthy guests' sensibilities, apparently. "When did she get here?"

"Who, red dress? Couple minutes ago…and she's talking to Lizzy. That woman has the hottest friends. Hell yeah, I think I might ask for an introduction later."

"Stay the fuck away from her," Kell growled before stalking in their direction.

He loved Vincent like a brother. They'd been in the Teams together and the other man had saved his ass more than once. After the Navy when Kell had joined the FBI, Vincent had started working for Red Stone Security. Now years later, Kell was with the same company, but he'd kick Vincent's ass if he ever made a move on Charlotte.

Coming to Miami had been a damn good career move, but right now the only thing he could focus on was the woman who'd stomped on his heart a year ago.

Not that he blamed her for how she'd reacted to what they'd done—fuck, he couldn't even go there right now. Couldn't even think about their history and how he'd messed things up so damn badly. All in one night, too. He'd completely screwed up a chance at even being friends with her when he'd made that stupid admission to her.

As he made his way through the room, circling around her, she must have felt his intense scrutiny. Though she was with Lizzy and two other women, she glanced over her shoulder, a relaxed expression on her pretty face—until she spotted him.

Though she was fair skinned, she paled even more as their gazes connected. Her dark brown eyes widened and she blinked twice, as if to make sure she'd actually seen him.

Oh yeah, sweetheart. It's me.

Taking him completely by surprise, she turned away from him, murmured something to one of the women, then practically sprinted into the crowd.

Away from him.

Even though he was hyper vigilant about the guests and his surroundings, Kell's gaze narrowed as he watched that fine ass run away. She'd never been a coward before so it shocked him that she was acting like one now. There was a lot of shit they needed to say to each other and while now clearly wasn't the place, he couldn't believe she'd actually tucked tail and run.

Not this time.

Rolling his shoulders once, he let her go. For now. He was working and wouldn't let anything get in the way of his job. But he'd damn sure find her before the night was over. Glancing around the expansive room, he surveyed some of the wealthiest people in Miami. Glittering jewels, pricey dresses and some of the most expensive art anywhere in the world was on display.

The Garcias wanted to show off their collection while throwing a thirty-five-year anniversary party. Anyone who was anyone in Miami was there. Kell had met Corinne Garcia and the sixty-year-old woman was eccentric and adorable. Standing a little under five feet tall, she'd married a man twice her size who looked fierce where she was soft and sweet. Somehow they fit. Together they'd accumulated a mass of wealth. Kell's job was to make sure there weren't any surprises tonight. There hadn't been any credible threats beforehand, but with all the art and jewels around, they weren't taking any chances with their safety or that of their guests. Something Kell respected. Some wealthy people became blind to the everyday threats facing them, but not the Garcia couple.

"You see something wrong?" Porter Caldwell, Lizzy's husband and one of his bosses, slid up next to him like a ghost.

Kell hated when he did that. But the former Marine moved like stealth personified. "No."

"Then what's wrong?"

"You know the woman in the red dress Lizzy was talking to earlier?"

Porter shrugged and grabbed a glass of champagne from a passing server. Unlike Kell, Porter wasn't working tonight. He might run Red Stone Security with his two brothers and father, but the man's wife came from serious wealth and they'd been invited as guests, not security. Still, Kell knew him well enough that Porter was definitely carrying a weapon and was watching the crowd. "Lizzy's parents know her parents. She's visiting from Virginia. Or maybe living here," he said distractedly, his gaze narrowing on the man walking up to Lizzy.

"You know why?" Kell asked, still scanning the room for any possible threats, but was thankful everything was calm and uneventful.

"Something to do with her kid. I don't know, I wasn't paying attention." Porter let out an annoyed sound, but Kell ignored it as he tried to digest what his friend had just said.

Kid? What the hell? Charlotte didn't have any children. Turning back to his boss, he gritted his teeth when he realized Porter had already melted into the crowd and was heading straight for his wife. The man in the expensive suit who'd been heading her way earlier was currently talking to her—and apparently Porter didn't like that. Ever since Lizzy had gotten pregnant Porter had been acting even more paranoid than normal. Not that he blamed the guy.

Sighing, Kell turned and slowly started making his way around the west side of the room. Porter must have been mistaken. Maybe he was talking about one of the other women Lizzy had been talking to—though there hadn't been any other women in red dresses he could have been referring to. Work came first and right now he needed to keep a sharp eye out for any possible threat. They weren't expecting any trouble, but he wouldn't let his guard down. Trying to shake that nagging feeling that something was off with Charlotte, Kell had reached the open French doors at the back of the house when someone spoke into his earpiece.

"Got a man secured by the back wall, but he's working with a partner. Male, five ten, dark hair, wearing a tux, heading toward the pool house," Travis, one of the other security guys, said, his words clipped.

"I'm on it. Those on perimeter stay put unless you see the suspect. Don't leave your posts." There were men and women placed all around the giant estate, and just in case this was a ploy to weaken their defense, he was taking this guy down himself. "Who's the closest to the pool house?" he asked as he hurried across the yard, disappearing in between a cluster of thick oak trees.

"I am." Iris Tarango's quiet voice came over the line. The tall, reed thin woman with clear Native American roots was deadly with a blade. He knew she'd been in the Marines and there were whispers that she'd been part of a secret intel-gathering group before coming to work for Red Stone, but that could all be bullshit. What he did know was that she was damn capable.

"I'll take the west side of the pool house, you take the east. If he's trying to scale the wall, he'll use the building as cover." Kell drew his weapon from his concealed shoulder holster, holding his SIG at the ready if he needed to use it.

There weren't supposed to be any guests this far back on the grounds so he wasn't worried about anyone seeing his weapon. Even if someone did he didn't care. He had a job to do. As he neared the pool area he slowed and ducked behind a tree, only peering out to scan the other trees and the pool house for threats. He wasn't actually worried about someone dropping down from the trees to assault him, but in his experience it was better to be prepared than end up ambushed.

He could hear a low, grunting and clanging sound so he eased out of his hiding place and hurried around the dimly lit pool to the one-story building. Slowly he crept along the wall and once he reached the end, he carefully looked around the corner.

For a moment he blinked at what he saw. A man in a tuxedo had a green hose with a nozzle on the end of it in his hands and was trying to throw it over the privacy wall like it had a grappling hook attached to it or something. Clearly these thieves hadn't thought anything through. Probably thought they'd do a quick grab and run.

Idiots.

Sheathing his weapon, Kell crept up on the man and tapped on his shoulder as he reached him. The man yelped and jumped as he turned. From his right Kell heard Iris snicker, but she didn't make her presence otherwise known.

"What are you doing?" he asked the other man calmly.

"Uh..." He looked around frantically and dropped the hose. As he moved a diamond bracelet fell out from somewhere under his jacket—he'd probably lifted it from a guest. The man stank of booze and even though he swayed once, he tried to take a swing at Kell.

Easily dodging the wide punch, Kell grabbed his arm, twisted him around and slammed his face against the wall as he pinned his arm behind his back. As the man struggled and cried out about 'suing his ass', Kell spoke into his communicator. "Got the other guy. Tell the police we'll be bringing them around the side of the house. They can pick them up near the main gate." He didn't want the guests seeing any of this.

Kell felt more than heard Iris as she approached. Wearing a sleek black dress that split to mid-thigh he knew she had to have a weapon on her somewhere. The woman rarely smiled but right now she was grinning. "I thought I was gonna die when you just tapped him on the shoulder like that. You should've just punched him."

His eyes widened slightly at her comment. "Didn't know you were so bloodthirsty."

She simply shrugged and the man he'd just flex-cuffed moaned about police brutality. "We're not the police you dick," Iris muttered as she grabbed one of his upper arms.

Kell took the other and they began leading him back toward the house. Oh yeah, tonight was off to a great start.

CHAPTER TWO

Five hours after handing the would-be jewel thieves over to the police, the party was winding down and most people had left. Throughout the night Kell had gotten flashes of that damn red dress. But Charlotte had done well at staying out of sight, clearly dodging him.

He hadn't seen her leave, though, so he'd switched posts with one of the men guarding the main entrance. She had to come this way sometime. As if on cue, she strode toward him, arms linked with a drunk-looking woman. An older woman—he recognized Charlotte's mother from photos—subtly held the intoxicated woman up on the other side as they slowly walked toward the giant front doors.

Their heels clicked along the marble entryway and though Charlotte wasn't looking at him, he knew she was very aware of him. Her posture was stiff and a flush had spread down her neck and chest. Though he could only see the outline of her breasts, he had a feeling that flush kept going and it made him remember how she'd looked as she climaxed underneath him. Feeling an uncomfortable tightening in his pants, he shifted and drew his gaze back up to her face.

Only to find her watching him warily.

As they neared, Charlotte murmured something to her mother, then dropped the other woman's arm and strode toward him, all liquid grace and sinful curves. He could almost believe she was unaffected, but he knew her too well. Her normally full lips were pulled into a tight line and there was worry in her dark eyes.

She cleared her throat as she stopped in front of him and clasped her hands tightly in front of herself. "Hi, Kell. I didn't expect to see you here."

His jaw clenched once as he tried to order himself to be nice. No matter how angry he was at the way she'd left things between them, he never wanted to cause her pain. "I gathered that from the way you ran away earlier."

Her cheeks flushed crimson, but she didn't look away or try to deny it. "Yeah...sorry about that. You surprised me and I sort of panicked."

He took a step closer, completely invading her personal space. Not that he cared. That sweet, familiar jasmine scent wrapped around him subtly, reminding him of too many things he tried to keep locked down. Unable to stop himself, he reached out and clasped her hip, tugging her closer. He didn't care that there were people around—namely some of the men he worked with—he just needed to touch her.

She let out a gasp at his possessive, bold move and he couldn't blame her. But hell, a year of not seeing her or getting to touch her and he felt damn near possessed with the need. The telling thing was that she didn't pull away.

It was subtle, but she gently shivered as he flexed his fingers around her hip. Oh yeah, she liked it when he got a little dominating. He was glad that hadn't changed. "You look good, Charlotte."

She swallowed hard and shook her head, as if trying to clear it. Then she came to her senses and stepped back, but not so far that he let go. "I'd like to see you tomorrow if possible. We need to talk."

Surprised by the abruptness of her words, he let his hand drop as he nodded. "When and where?" He had the day off, but even if he hadn't, he'd have taken it off. They needed to set things straight.

She looked down at her clasped hands for a moment and when she met his gaze again he saw such a raw vulnerability there that it struck him like a body blow. "Maybe your place? I'm staying with my parents until I get a home of my own and—"

"You're living in Miami?" Oh, hell yeah.

She nodded, a foreign emotion he couldn't define in her eyes. She looked almost scared. Of him? No, he immediately rejected the thought. "How about nine? If that's too early—"

"Nine works. I'll give you my address."

"I already have it."

Now it was his turn to be surprised. "You do?"

She nodded again. "I'm in Miami to see you."

His chest constricted with so many unsaid things, but she still looked scared and he refused to believe it was because of him. Something else had to be going on. "What the hell is wrong? Are you in trouble? You know I'll help any way I can." There wasn't much he wouldn't do for this woman no matter how much time had passed.

Her expression softened. "I know—"

"Hurry up, Charlotte, I'm not waitin' all night for you and your baby's daddy." The drunk woman, maybe her sister, slurred out as Charlotte's mother struggled to hold her up.

Kell blinked suddenly as the words registered, his gaze snapping back to Charlotte who'd gone deathly pale. Baby? She actually had a baby? She looked horrified that he knew.

And she also wasn't denying what the woman had said. Instead she placed a soft hand on his chest, that vulnerable look back in her eyes, her smile strained. "Tomorrow at nine?"

Feeling numb, he nodded. Had Charlotte had his baby? They'd used plenty of condoms that night...but she'd definitely changed since he'd seen her a year ago. Her body was slightly fuller, her breasts just a bit rounder. But what the woman had said had to be *impossible*. His brain refused to comprehend what she'd said.

No, just...no.

He wanted to demand answers, to leave with her right then or drag her off somewhere private. But when he realized Vincent was watching him curiously, he stepped back and let them leave. He watched as the valet driver handed the keys to a newer model Bentley to Charlotte's mother before helping Charlotte get the other woman into the backseat.

An hour later the place had cleared out and the team had secured the perimeter and home, making sure there weren't any stragglers left behind. The homeowners had regular security guys and a state of the art alarm system they would activate once the Red Stone team left, but they never did a half-assed job.

Finally Kell found himself in the backseat of one of Red Stone's company SUVs headed away from Star Island and back into the heart of downtown Miami where his truck waited. He felt as if he was moving on autopilot, practically numb to the news that he might be a father. It was too surreal. Seconds after Charlotte had left he realized he had no way to contact her other than email. She'd changed her number months ago and he couldn't stand the thought of waiting until nine to talk to her. It was only six hours away but it seemed like an eternity.

"So...is what that woman said true? You have a kid?" Vincent asked from his seat next to him.

The driver, Travis, muttered under his breath that Vincent was a jackass and the other passenger, some new guy, laughed quietly.

Kell's jaw clenched. "I don't know." But he was damn sure going to find out.

Vincent's eyebrows rose. "Damn. All right, you want to grab a drink?"

"Leave the man alone," Travis muttered.

Kell shook his head. "No, but thanks for the offer." He might have no clue what was going on, but he sure as hell wanted his head on straight for when he saw Charlotte. If she'd kept the existence of his child from him she better have a damn good reason.

CHAPTER THREE

Charlotte wiped a damp palm on her jeans before ringing the doorbell. Kell lived in a very quiet middle class neighborhood in a cottage style home so typical of Miami. It was nine a.m. exactly, but she was still surprised when the door swung open immediately. He'd clearly been waiting for her.

Not that she should be shocked about that. Not after her big-mouthed, drunk sister's comment last night. God, what had Allison been thinking saying that out loud?

He was going to have questions and would probably—no, definitely—be angry with her. Kell had never been easygoing. Out of all her deceased husband's friends with the FBI, he'd always been the serious one. He had such a dark edge to him that when she thought of how gentle he'd been with her the night they—gah, she couldn't even go there. Just thinking about that night made her ready to melt into a puddle at his feet.

He was tall with shorter dark hair, a forbidding expression and broad shoulders she still wanted to run her fingers across just to feel all his strength. Sighing, she cursed how good he looked. She'd tried to convince herself that she'd simply built up his hotness in her mind. No such luck. He was still gorgeous. Of course she was still hanging onto ten pounds of post-pregnancy weight, and he looked like a Greek god. And those eyes—the same pale green as her son. The doctor told her that his eye color could change by his first birthday as with all babies, but she knew better.

Charlotte knew that eye color was there to stay.

With a hard stare, he wordlessly stepped back, gesturing with his hand and very muscular outstretched arm that she should enter. She *so* did not want to be doing this, but she had no choice. Her sandals made soft slapping sounds against the hardwood floor on his foyer. When he shut the door behind them and she heard the soft click of the lock, she felt as if she might suffocate. Her stomach muscles were pulled tight in dread.

Until he spoke. "I have a fresh pot of coffee in the kitchen if you want some."

That deep voice rolled over her like a tidal wave, evoking too many long-buried emotions. He didn't sound angry, but his voice wasn't friendly either. It was reserved.

She needed to keep it together. At least long enough to get out everything she had to say. Then she could have an emotional breakdown on the way back to her parents' house. "That sounds great."

Surprising her, he placed a gentle hand at the small of her back and led her down a short hallway into a brightly lit kitchen painted a soft robin's egg blue. The room was cheery, but still masculine.

"Why don't you sit." It wasn't a question. He motioned to a ladder-back, white-washed chair at a center island. "Still take your coffee with two creams, no sugar?"

"Yes." That one word came out shaky, but she couldn't control it. She was nervous over his reaction to the fact that he was a father.

After he filled both their mugs and sat in front of her, she could see that he was about to talk. But if he started, she'd never get out what she needed to. Hell, she'd been trying to work up the courage to see him for weeks.

Here goes nothing. "I had a baby three months ago. He's yours." When Kell swallowed hard, she wondered if he thought she was lying. The thought made her frown. "We'll do a paternity test, but I can guarantee he's yours." She hadn't even slept with her husband four months before he'd died so there wasn't even a question. "I wanted to tell you earlier. God, I wanted to tell you so bad, but I was high risk and on bed rest my entire pregnancy. My doctor was very adamant that I have no stress in my life, and you and I..." Well, he knew how they'd left things. After he'd said three little words she'd freaked out and kicked him out of her house and her life. Months later, she'd realized she was pregnant.

He just sat there, his expression blank as he listened. Which made this so much harder.

But she continued. "I should have told you right after he was born but I just couldn't. I'm a coward and I freely admit that. The first six weeks I was barely sleeping or eating and just trying to be a new mom. I couldn't bring a new baby into your life until I'd gotten ahold of this whole motherhood thing. And for the last six weeks I've been working up the courage to tell you. I just want you to know I don't expect anything from you, but if you'd like to be involved we'll work out a custody agreement. I know what kind of man you are and our son deserves to have both parents in his life. This is a hell of a lot to lay on you at once, I know that, so don't think you have to answer now. Just know that I don't expect child support or anything. But you have a right to know so...here I am." She wished he'd just interrupt her or something! He was simply listening intently and she couldn't stop rambling. It was like she had verbal diarrhea.

He hadn't taken those pale green eyes off her once and it was wildly unnerving. Finally he spoke. "What's his name?"

She blinked, surprised he hadn't mentioned anything about paternity. "Reece."

Now it was his turn to blink. "You named him after my brother?"

Charlotte nodded. His brother had died in Afghanistan years ago and he'd been Kell's only living family.

Kell rubbed a hand over his face and shifted against his seat restlessly. "Can I see him today?"

"Of course. I would have brought him, but..." Shrugging, she trailed off. "Don't you want to do a paternity test first?"

He snorted. "When was the last time you slept with Andrew before he died?"

Damn. "Not pulling any punches today, huh?"

"Should I be after your sister dropped that bomb on me last night?" he asked quietly.

Fair enough. "Maybe four months, probably a little longer," she rasped out, embarrassed. Despite what her family had thought about her supposedly perfect marriage, she and her husband had been on a path straight for divorce. He'd been distant for almost a year before he died, blaming it on his job, but she'd suspected the truth. He'd been seeing someone. Looking down at her hands, she swallowed the shame. She hadn't even been able to keep her husband happy enough not to stray.

"It wasn't your fault," Kell bit out.

Her head snapped up at the quiet words. "You knew he was cheating?"

He nodded once, his expression tight.

Rage popped inside her like fireworks. Kell had known? Of course he had. Probably everyone with the FBI's Hostage Rescue Team had. Those guys were all like brothers and they all stuck together. "Of course you did," she muttered in disgust. She wasn't angry at him, but the entire situation.

"I wanted to tell you." There was a raw honesty in his voice that surprised her.

She ignored it and focused on the present. "It's not important." And it wasn't something she wanted to talk about with Kell again. Ever. "I guess I expected a little resistance or something, but whenever you want to see Reece, you're welcome to. If you want to come over now, that works, but... I'm not giving him up fifty percent of the time. He's too young and I've been his whole world. I want you in his life, but I just can't change his life like that." The truth was, she wasn't worried about that anyway. She was pretty certain Kell wouldn't try to do that to her, but she also knew how much the courts favored mothers in situations like this—her parents had looked into it and had wanted to hire an expensive lawyer but she'd told them to back off. She was fairly sure that she and Kell could work things out amicably.

"Why are you living with your parents?" His question surprised her, but she supposed it was fair.

"Now that I have Reece I wanted to be closer to my family and DC holds too many memories. I have no family there, the cost of living is terrible and," she shrugged, "I can teach anywhere. I only moved there for Andrew anyway. This is my hometown and I missed it. I couldn't believe it when I found out you'd taken a job here." It had almost seemed like fate—if she believed in that kind of crap anymore.

"I can't believe you didn't tell me I had a son sooner." There was a bite of anger in his words that didn't surprise her. He was almost preternaturally still, the anger pulsing off him in waves.

Sitting there, she prepared herself for whatever he'd throw at her. When she'd admitted to Andrew's parents that their 'perfect' son wasn't the father of her unborn child they'd called her all sorts of names. Her old friends in DC had been shocked she'd gotten pregnant with another man's child so soon after her husband's death. God, she could just imagine what Kell had to say to her now. Yes, they'd used condoms, but clearly one of them had broken. It wasn't like she'd planned it, but for all she knew he could accuse her of getting pregnant intentionally. She nearly snorted at the ludicrousness of that thought.

"You're moving in with me."

Her eyes widened at his statement. "Excuse me?"

"I've already lost three months of my son's life. I would never try to take him away from you, but I deserve to spend time with him. I'm not saying this is permanent, but I want him here. With me. I want to see my son every day when I wake up and when I come home at night. I deserve that." His voice was heated.

Charlotte swallowed back the tears. Kell was such a good, caring man and a dark, very small part of her was a little jealous he wasn't saying he wanted to see *her* every morning and evening. Which was stupid considering she didn't want a relationship with him—or any man for that matter. "That's insane, Kell. Babies are a lot of work. Sleepless nights, teething, crying—"

"Exactly. And I've had to miss out on all of that for three months."

Because of you. He didn't say the words, but she could hear them hovering in the air. "So you seriously want me and Reece to move in with you?"

"It's happening."

She gritted her teeth. She hated when he got all bossy like that. Scrubbing a hand over her face, she sighed. Her first instinct was to say hell no, but the guilt swamping her over how she'd waited so long to tell him about Reece was stomping on that instinct. "What about your job or social life or girlfriend...?" She struggled to come up with more excuses, but just the thought of him having a girlfriend or even dating anyone clawed at her insides.

"None of that will be a problem." Okay, he hadn't exactly answered if he had a girlfriend or not. "This will be a temporary thing. All I'm asking for is three months and I think that's fair considering what I've lost. It'll give you time to find a place to live and after that we'll figure out a shared agreement that works for you."

"Three months, then we figure out a permanent solution?" The one thing she wasn't worried about was Kell being a good father to Reece. The man was loyal and giving and would do anything he could to protect and care for their son. She was just worried about what being under the same roof as Kell would do to her heart.

There was something in his gaze she couldn't define as he said, "Yep." He crossed his arms over his chest, looking fierce and demanding.

Guilt was a huge factor pushing her into this, but the truth was her loud and usually drunk sister had just moved back into her parent's house and she didn't want her son around that mess. Not even for a little bit. She'd looked at a few places but they hadn't been in areas she was comfortable living with a small child. She knew she was going to regret it, but... "Okay."

CHAPTER FOUR

Kell waited impatiently in his foyer, trying to force himself to stop pacing. His heart was beating out of control as he imagined seeing and holding his son for the first time. He knew what he'd done was slightly dirty, playing on Charlotte's guilt, but he didn't give a damn. Though the thought of being a father scared the hell out of him, he wanted desperately to meet his son. He was supposed to be sent off for two weeks on an out-of-town security job, but he'd talked to his boss and worked things out so he could stay local for the next month—at least. There were so many things he and Charlotte needed to figure out, but the only thing he could focus on now was keeping both her and...his son close to him.

His throat tightened as he tried to wrap his head around the fact that he was suddenly a dad. His own father had been a violent alcoholic so Kell had basically raised his brother after their mom died. He knew more about babies than Charlotte probably realized.

At the sound of a car door shutting, he threw open his front door and strode outside. He hadn't thought she'd be back so soon, especially since she'd be bringing over so many things for Reece. He'd wanted to go and help but she'd been adamant that she deal with her parents by herself. Considering how stubborn she could be, Kell knew when to pick his battles. As long as Charlotte didn't change her mind about moving in, he could give her space.

When he saw Monique, the blonde with legs a mile long he'd gone on a couple dates with get out of her two-door sports car he froze, his excitement dying. What the hell was she doing here?

She gave him a little half wave as she strode toward him. Wearing a black skintight mini dress and high heels, she was almost as tall as him. "Hey, Kell." Her voice was practically a purr.

"Hey, what are you doing here?"

She shrugged. "I was in the neighborhood, thought I'd stop by."

He glanced at the road, which was thankfully empty of vehicles. The thought of Charlotte driving up now made him feel sick. Before she'd left, the indecision in her gaze had been clear and he wouldn't let anything get in the way of her moving in with him. As she was leaving to get their son she'd mentioned that her alcoholic sister was now living with her parents too so he had a feeling that her acquiescence to move in was part guilt, part not wanting Reece to be around her sister. He'd let Charlotte run from him a year ago because her world had crashed down on her head and he hadn't wanted to add to her problems.

Now things were different. He wasn't some fucking rebound or a way to make herself feel guilty.

"It's not a good time."

Monique placed a well-manicured hand on his chest, her expression pouty. "Why not?"

Kell bit back his nausea. He didn't want anyone touching him but Charlotte. A few months ago he'd tried to purge her from his system by dating Monique, but it hadn't worked. They'd gotten physical but he hadn't been able to sleep with her. Not when he kept picturing Charlotte's face. It had felt beyond wrong. "Because I'm seeing someone."

Her blue eyes narrowed, the intensity of her anger surprising him. "Since when?"

"Since now. Why the hell are you here?"

She shrugged and curled her hand against his chest. He took her wrist and removed it as gently as he could. She still didn't walk away. "Saw you at the Garcia party last night."

He frowned, not remembering seeing her there. "You were invited to the party?"

She shrugged again in that annoying way of hers. As she did, a compact SUV pulled up to the curb outside his house.

Charlotte.

"You need to leave. Now." He kept his expression blank, trying to will the other woman to get the hell off his property. Right now everything with Charlotte was so tentative he didn't want to screw things up before he had a chance to make his intentions clear. He knew she planned on sleeping in one of his guestrooms, but he planned on making that a short term thing. He wanted her in his bed and his life permanently.

Monique glanced over her shoulder, then glared back at him. "Fine. See you later." With an obnoxious wave to Charlotte, Monique slid into her car and zoomed away.

Kell strode for Charlotte's vehicle. He was surprised when she got out and rounded it, fury and hurt written on her face. She had her keys gripped tightly in a fist as she practically squared off with him. She wore the same jeans and green sweater, which did nothing to hide the outline of her generous breasts. "This isn't going to work, Kell. I'm not going to introduce my son to a bunch of strange women."

He tried to bite back his fury. Way to jump to conclusions. "That woman means nothing and she's not coming back."

Her jaw tightened as she stared at him, and all he could think about was kissing away that anger. Then she shook her head. "You can spend a couple hours with Reece, but this isn't going to work. I knew it was a mistake when I said yes. We can't—"

Unable to listen to one more word, he moved fast, covering the few steps between them in seconds until he was on her. His hand fisted in her hair, gripping the back of her head as he crushed his mouth over hers.

She let out a strangled moan into his mouth and for a moment he thought she'd shove him away. He wouldn't blame her if she did. He was pushing too fast. When her fingers twisted into his shirt, tugging him closer, he knew he'd won for the moment. Sweeping his tongue past the seam of her lips, he didn't give her a chance to resist. He kissed her hard and dominating, the way he wanted to fuck her. The need to take this woman, to slake his never-ending lust around her, was a primal, living thing inside him. From the moment he'd met her it had been like that for him. Unfortunately she'd been very taken. So he'd ignored her as best he could, but it had become damn near impossible when she was one of the sweetest women he'd ever met. Now that she was the mother of his child, his need to claim her was even stronger.

Breaking the moment, Charlotte shoved at him, wrenching her head back. "What was that for?"

"That woman is nothing to me and no woman is going to be in our son's or my life now except you. I don't want any woman but *you*," he growled, unable to stop the admission. Her eyes were wide and definitely surprised. Still gripping her, he loosened his hold and slid his hand around to cup her cheek and neck. He could feel her pulse pounding out of control.

"Kellen, this is a mistake," she whispered, suddenly looking exhausted.

God, he loved it when she said his full name. He wasn't sure if she meant the kiss or her coming there, but he didn't care which. Neither were. He knew it. She just needed time to see it herself. Dropping his hand to give her a little space, he looked over her shoulder into the interior of the vehicle. He could see the outline of the car seat, but it was turned away from the window. Excitement and nervousness punched through him in equal waves. He couldn't believe he was about to see his son for the first time. "Is he in there?"

At the question, Charlotte's entire face softened. She nodded. "Yeah. Sleeping."

His heart beat faster at the thought of holding his son. "You managed to pack all your things in this vehicle?" The mini SUV had decent storage but he'd expected her to have a lot more stuff, especially for a baby.

She snorted, the sound irreverent and totally Charlotte. "No. My dad is hiring someone to bring over everything. They should be here in a few hours, but..." She trailed off, biting her lip.

That was when he realized what she meant. "No buts. You said you'd try this temporarily."

"I know, I'm just worried you're not prepared. Reece doesn't sleep through the night yet and—"

"I practically raised my brother." Kell had been ten when his brother had been born and his mother had died a year later. He knew all about kids.

Rubbing a hand over her face, she sighed. "Okay, let me get him out of his seat."

He waited impatiently on the curb as Charlotte pulled the small, sleeping baby with a thick mass of dark hair from the car seat. She cuddled him close to her chest, her expression soft as she watched their son.

Their. Son.

He moved closer, hovering behind her to get a better look at Reece and his heart melted. The sight of Charlotte holding Reece made it difficult to think straight for a moment.

"He'll probably be out for another hour. He ate right before we left," she said quietly.

As if to prove her wrong, those little eyes snapped open and Kell's breath caught. Not that he'd ever worried about Charlotte lying about the paternity, but he knew right then and there, without a doubt, that this was his son. He saw those same eyes every day he looked in the mirror.

The little boy looked at his mother, then him, then back to her. His tiny mouth opened and he let out the loudest cry Kell had ever heard. The sound pierced the quiet neighborhood as his face turned bright red. It also pierced his heart and made him feel useless to hear his son upset. A small being shouldn't be able to make that kind of sound.

Charlotte just snorted. "He's hungry again. Greedy little thing. I'm going to feed him inside." With that, she carried Reece up his driveway and into his house.

Kell wanted to follow immediately but he sagged against the vehicle and tried to catch his breath. Knowing that he had a son and actually seeing the little boy were two different things. Unable to fight the grin on his face, he started gathering bags from the back of the vehicle. He wondered how soon it would be before he got to hold the little guy. No matter what, he was going to be the kind of father that he'd never had.

* * *

Charlotte slipped on a pair of comfortable yoga pants and a nursing tank top before heading out of the guestroom to find Reece and Kell. Kell had told her to shower and sleep and she'd decided to take advantage. Her family hadn't been much help with Reece because they'd dealing with her sister's antics, so getting even a small break was like heaven. She'd been able to shower, shave and actually put on a little makeup, making her feel like a woman again instead of just a mom. Kell had been so eager and excited to hold Reece it had been easier than she'd imagined to give them alone time.

The men her father had hired had dropped off Reece's bedroom furniture and all of her clothes a couple hours ago. She still had to unpack some boxes and hang up her clothes, but they truly didn't have much. Luckily Kell didn't have a lot of furniture in either guestroom so their moving in wasn't an issue.

When she'd left DC she'd sold all their furniture and purged almost everything she'd owned with her husband. She'd needed a fresh start and hadn't wanted any reminders of her life with him. He'd hurt her enough with his lies and cheating. She deserved better. More importantly, so did her son.

Despite her nervousness about moving in here with Kell, she smiled when she stepped into the living room. Kell was leaning back on his couch, his feet kicked up on the coffee table as he watched a football game. The volume was so low she could barely hear it. And Reece was tucked perfectly in the crook of his arm, sleeping soundly.

"How'd he do?"

Kell grinned, supremely satisfied with himself. "Perfect. He fussed a little over the bottle at first but took it after a few tries."

She'd pumped extra milk for him so she could nap. "Good. You can turn the television up, you know. He's used to noise. It's good for him anyway."

Kell's eyebrows pulled together in concern. "You're sure?"

Fighting a grin, she nodded. "Yes. Trust me, you want this kid able to sleep through anything. It will save your sanity later. Are you hungry? Because I'm starving. I'll cook." Since Reece was clearly content, she wanted to keep her hands busy and keep her distance from Kell. Not because she didn't like his company. If anything, she craved it too much and that was dangerous.

"Yeah, but we can order takeout."

She shook her head. "No, I'll cook. Before I do I want to go over some rules." Including a very important one.

His eyebrows quirked up as he slightly straightened. "Rules?"

"That's right. One, I'll be paying you rent." When it looked like he was about to argue she shook her head. "I'm going to be a contributing member of this household. With my savings, my trust fund and Andrew's life insurance, I'm more than capable." Some days she felt guilty that she didn't have to work—though as soon as Reece entered preschool she was going back to teaching—but the fact that she was able to stay home with her son squashed all those feelings. "Second, no more kissing. Once this arrangement ends I don't want there to be any confusion for either of us. Third, if I'm doing something you don't like or something that annoys you, tell me right away. We've got a baby in the house and we're two adults who've been on our own for a while. This will take some adjustment and I'm all about getting things out in the open so there's no resentment. Okay?"

After a long moment, he nodded. "Those are good rules—except number two. I won't promise not to kiss you again."

She gritted her teeth. "Kell—"

"You liked it," he murmured, his voice all sin and seduction as it rolled over her. And his expression was heated and almost smug—because it was the truth.

She had liked it. Way too much. Hell, she'd gotten wet from a simple kiss. Of course nothing about that kiss had been simple. It had been hot and dominating. And she knew from experience just how much Kell liked to dominate. But she couldn't deal with that right now. Not if she wanted to stay sane and in control. "That's beside the point. We can't have things get complicated when we have no chance of something long term."

His green eyes narrowed. "And why is that?"

She rolled her eyes, refusing to be baited. He knew exactly why. She'd been married to one of his friends. Then a month after her husband had died she'd found out about his cheating. She'd had her suspicions before but to her horror, she'd gotten them confirmed by one of his mistresses. Of course that was the night Kell had decided to show up to check on her. So she'd jumped him in an effort to drown her pain and get back at a man who was dead—then the next morning Kell had said he loved her. She still wished she could erase that from her memory. There was no way it was true. The man was too much of a player and she wasn't going down that road again. Her heart couldn't take it.

She sighed. "Kell, I know what you're like and while I adore you, neither of us are cut out for relationships." It had been part of the reason she'd picked him for a one-night stand. She'd liked and trusted him and had assumed he wouldn't want more than a night. Then he'd gone and shocked the hell out of her. And she hadn't been able to deal. Because if there was even a small chance he'd been serious...no, just no. She absolutely could not deal with that right now.

He straightened a little, anger glinting in his eyes. "And what exactly am I like?" He bit the words out.

She swallowed hard, his fierce expression surprising her. It wasn't like she was saying anything that wasn't true. "Don't forget that I knew you before we slept together."

"And?" One dark eyebrow arched in defiance.

God, was he going to make her spell it out? Reece shifted slightly in his arms and they both froze. When he didn't wake up, she let out a breath of relief.

"And...you're a player. I'm not judging, but come on, don't pretend—"

"Just stop," he ground out. "I don't give a shit what I was like before you, I'm not your dead fucking husband and I've never cheated on a girlfriend. I haven't actually slept with anyone since you either." When she started to roll her eyes at the absurdity, his intense look stopped her. "I tried—with that woman you saw in the driveway. It was a while ago, and I simply couldn't fuck someone else when all I could see was your face. When all I wanted to do was bury myself inside *you*."

Her breath caught in her throat when she realized he was completely serious. Since she couldn't even think about dwelling on what he'd just admitted, she decided not to comment directly. After living with her husband, she'd gotten pretty damn good at weeding out lies. Kell was telling the truth and that scared her. "Why was she here?"

At that, he looked frustrated. "I have no idea, but it won't be happening again."

"Okay."

"Okay, what?"

"I mean I believe you. But that still doesn't mean you're ignoring rule number two." She couldn't deal with a relationship right now. Absolutely not.

Kell laughed under his breath and as he did, Reece stirred and opened his eyes. When he saw her he started cooing and wiggling. Probably time for a diaper change then feeding. It was like a vicious cycle. And one she wouldn't give up for anything. Without her having to ask, Kell handed him to her. When Reece immediately went for her breast, she started to unclip the snap on her nursing top, but stopped when she realized Kell wasn't giving her any privacy. "Do you mind?"

"I've seen them before," he murmured, his voice holding a mischievous quality that should have frustrated her.

"Fine." Let him see how non-sexy she was right now. Maybe it would help convince him there was never going to be anything between them. But as she pulled her top down, for the briefest moment before Reece latched on, Kell's eyes flashed with pure lust. Just as quickly, he shoved up from his seat and strode from the room, leaving her feeling more confused than ever.

How the hell was she going to keep her sanity while living with him?

CHAPTER FIVE

Kell strode down the sidewalk toward Red Stone's building in the business district. He hadn't wanted to go to work today, but Charlotte had made it pretty damn clear he would be. Hell, she'd been insistent. Part of him was annoyed, but he knew he was getting under her skin.

All part of his plan to get her to realize they were meant for each other. Last night he'd intentionally walked around with his shirt off and he hadn't missed those covert looks she'd given him. Wide-eyed, full of lust and hunger before she quickly shut down and turned away from him.

He still couldn't believe she was living in the same city, much less under his roof, but he wasn't going to balk at this second chance.

"Kell, wait up!" He turned to see Travis, another Red Stone employee, jogging down the sidewalk.

While he didn't know Travis that well, Vincent and him were tight, and since Kell trusted Vincent's opinion on most things that didn't involve women, he figured the guy was all right. The Garcia party was the only job they'd actually worked together so Kell didn't know what he was like in the field in a large scale sense.

Standing on the sidewalk, he gave a half-nod to the tattooed former Marine. "What's up?"

Travis had a covered Styrofoam cup of coffee in one hand and two brownies wrapped in cellophane in the other. He handed him the brownies. "Noel said you left these at the shop."

Shit. He'd stopped at the local coffee shop that almost everyone in the business district frequented for a quick lunch, and had been so distracted by thoughts of Charlotte he'd forgotten what he'd bought for her. The woman had a wicked sweet tooth. "Thanks, man."

Travis grunted a response then tilted his head toward Red Stone and they resumed walking. "You working local right now?"

"Yeah, Harrison's got me doing only local stuff the next few weeks." Because he'd requested it so he could be near Charlotte—but he didn't tell the other guy that.

"Me too. Makes Noel happy."

He knew Travis was recently engaged to the coffee shop owner, but that was about all. "I bet." He also knew it made Travis happy too.

The travel was the only downside to this job for anyone in a relationship, but most spouses of Red Stone's employees dealt with it well. They had to or their relationships would tank. *Relationships.* He nearly snorted at the word. Overnight he'd gone from missing a woman so bad he ached for her on a daily basis to living under the same roof as her and their son. But they weren't in a relationship.

Not yet.

He needed to keep his shit together if he was going to make sure Charlotte and Reece *stayed* under his roof. His phone buzzed in his pocket. When he saw Charlotte's name on the caller ID he felt like a horny teenager with his first crush. Yeah, way to keep it together.

* * *

Charlotte tucked Reece's blue and white blanket tighter around his little body as they stopped on the sidewalk next to Lummus Park. Of the two parks with the same name, the one in South Beach was her favorite. All the greenery, wide sidewalks and historic views of the art deco style buildings across from the beach/park area made her feel as if she'd stepped back into 1950s Miami. She loved all the older model cars lining the street, especially the 1958 Pontiac Bonneville Sport Coupe sitting in front of the Avalon Hotel she'd been in love with since she was a teenager. Yeah, she'd definitely missed Miami. Coming back here was the best decision she could have made for her and her son.

After being confined under the same roof as Kell all day yesterday she'd needed the fresh air and to get out of that house. He'd wanted to call in for a personal day at work, but she'd convinced him not to. While he'd been amazing and loving with Reece they needed to keep their lives as normal as possible. Plus, the thought of spending an entire day with him was too much for her already frayed nerves. Once they'd gotten Reece to bed last night Kell had showered and decided to walk around wearing lounge pants and no shirt.

It was his house and it wasn't like she could tell him to put clothes on, especially when she had a feeling he hadn't intentionally been trying to tempt her with that hot body. Unfortunately that was exactly what he'd done anyway. All those sleek muscles and defined striations just reminded her of how amazing things had been between them on a physical level. It had only been one night, but he'd been so giving. When she'd made that first move on him, it was like she'd unleashed something in him. Looking back she realized he'd clearly had feelings for her *before* that night. At the time it hadn't registered. She thought she'd just been another warm body for him. But a man didn't spend all night pleasuring a woman like that if he didn't have feelings for her. She'd assumed they could both take what they needed and walk away. If only life was that easy.

For the last half of her pregnancy and the last three months, her sexual needs had been dormant. Half the time she felt like a feeding machine, like her body wasn't even her own.

Until Kell was suddenly back in her life.

Now she felt alive again and was utterly confused about that. She didn't want to want him. She didn't want to want *anybody*. After Andrew's betrayal, yeah, she couldn't even go there. Sighing, she turned the stroller around and headed back toward Lincoln Road. She was meeting her mom for lunch at a tapas restaurant and knew she'd have to feed Reece before she got there, but she'd wanted to get some walking in before they met. The fresh air was good for her son. The walk was quiet and despite the cooler February weather, a few people zoomed by on bikes wearing shorts and T-shirts.

When Reece opened his eyes, blearily looked around and started that murmured cooing sound she recognized too well, she crossed the street and found a quiet bench in front of one of the historic hotels. As she finished up feeding Reece, she started to put him back in his stroller when she heard loud, frantic shouting coming from the side alley next to the hotel.

Her son had already dozed again, his head resting against her breast, clearly not disturbed by the noises. The boy could sleep through anything, which was a minor miracle. Though she wanted to ignore the shouts they were getting more panicked by the second. Pulling out her smartphone to call for help if necessary, she kept Reece tucked against her body and strode down the sidewalk to where the alley opened up. She just wanted to peek around and see if calling the police was necessary. This was a very quiet, safe area so she doubted it, but she wanted to be prepared.

What she saw made her freeze. Two men, one blond, one with dark hair, were arguing heatedly with a younger Hispanic man probably in his twenties. He was holding his hands up defensively while the dark haired one held a gun loosely at his side. Panic punched through her at the sight of the weapon. The blond bit something out in a sharp tone, then lunged forward, pulling the Hispanic man to his chest.

Oh God, he'd stabbed him. The realization slammed into her, forcing her legs into action as she stepped back and out of sight. That was a dead end alley which meant they'd have to come back this way. She had to get Reece away from this. Had to keep her son safe.

With her heart pounding wildly, she hurried back the few yards to her stroller and began pushing it down the sidewalk as fast as she could. Still holding her son, she knew how frantic she must look. The traffic was too thick to cross to the other side and if she stopped to put Reece in his seat and they saw her they might guess she'd seen them.

Hoping it was the right decision, she glanced over her shoulder then sat on another bench farther away from the alley. She yanked her nursing cover from the stroller and hooked the strap over her head and covered Reece. He was asleep so it looked like she was just breastfeeding. Then she held her phone up to her ear and dialed Kell. She knew he'd be smart enough to help her without her having to spell everything out.

"Hey," he answered on the first ring.

"Yeah, mom, just running a little late. Had to stop and feed the baby." She tried for a light laugh but it came out brittle and strained.

There was a brief pause in which she heard male voices trailing somewhere behind her. She refused to look over her shoulder as she prayed they ignored her and kept walking. "Where are you?" Kell's voice was tense.

"Not far at all, just across from Lummus Park near Avalon. I'll be there in ten minutes, twenty tops."

"Can you tell me what's going on?"

"No, he'll be done soon." The voices behind her had stopped but she could see the dark haired man out of the corner of her eye walking in her direction. Her arms tightened around Reece's sleeping form. Oh God, she was going to throw up.

"Is Reece safe?"

"For right now." She would fight these men until her last breath to keep her son safe.

"I'm on my way. Can you stay on the phone?"

"Sure, I love that tapas place." The man was moving closer, closer... He paused by the sidewalk and looked at her. Praying she didn't look guilty, she shot the man a quick glance and smiled politely.

He smiled back, the action tight and suspicious and he frowned when he seemed to finally notice the lump under her cover. Holding the phone down for a second, she tapped into an inner strength she didn't know she had as she held eye contact. A woman who'd just witnessed a murder wouldn't talk to said murderer, now would she? "Sorry, the little one got hungry. Hope this doesn't bother you."

He just shook his head politely, relief flooding his expression as he looked over her at someone behind her and shook his head. She could only guess he was motioning to the blond man. Her nausea swelled to epic proportions as she tried to keep her breakfast down. When the man turned away, some of the terror forking through her seeped out—until she saw the bright, shiny gold badge flash under the man's jacket as he twisted away from her. Holy shit. He was a cop.

"No, mom, I promise, I'll be there soon." She felt numb as she continued rambling. Kell was mostly silent, only telling her he'd be in her area soon and that everything was going to be okay. His voice was the only thing steadying her, the only thing keeping her sane when all she wanted to do was have a breakdown. As soon as the dark-haired man reached the park side of the street and got into a four-door car and pulled away from the curb, she took a risk and glanced over her shoulder. The blond man had to have gone that way.

The hair on the back of her neck was prickling and she knew she was probably being crazy, but she had to see if he was gone. There were a couple women with shopping bags walking her way, but the blond was leaning against the front of a shutdown hotel the next block over. He was far enough away, but not so far that she couldn't make out his face clearly.

And he was watching her intently.

She tried to hide her expression, the knowledge that she knew must be in her eyes, but he locked on her in that moment, straightening from the wall and pure terror shot through her. He took a determined step toward her, his face murderous. Holding Reece tight, she jumped from the bench, looked left, then ran into the road and started screaming at the top of her lungs for help. There were no cars coming from the west and the one from the east slammed on the brakes, forcing the line of cars behind him to stop. The two people across the street at the park jumped into action, racing toward her.

Too many things were happening at once. At least Reece hadn't stirred.

"Charlotte! Charlotte!" She could hear her name being shouted and realized it was coming from her phone. She held it loosely by her side as she glanced over her shoulder.

The blond man was running down the street away from her. Suddenly the man from the stopped car was out and in front of her.

"Ma'am! What's going on?"

"I saw a man murdered," she said both to Kell and the stranger. "Call the police, now. He's in that alley." She motioned with her head, before hurrying the rest of the way across the street to where more people had gathered from the park on the sidewalk. Reece was now moving against her, his eyes open. He started making gurgling sounds with his lips, trying to blow raspberries and just drooling as he watched her happily.

Nothing should have been able to make her smile in that moment, but her son was alive, unharmed and completely oblivious to what had just happened. Her knees were weak with terror and she couldn't stop shaking, but her son was okay. She had to remind herself of that.

Charlotte might hate being part of any spectacle, but there was safety in numbers and for once she was incredibly grateful for the gathering crowd of park and beach-goers.

"Honey, can you talk now? What's going on?"

Charlotte quickly filled Kell in, more relief flooding her when she heard sirens in the distance. The only thing she held back from telling Kell was the fact that one of the men she'd seen had been a cop. She didn't want anyone overhearing that. When he got there she'd tell him everything and let him figure out what to do. Last night when they'd talked about the company he now worked for, he'd mentioned they had a lot of former local law enforcement working for them, including one of the owners. She'd accept his judgment on this because there was no way in hell she was trusting this knowledge to anyone else. Especially not the police.

CHAPTER SIX

Kell felt as if his heart was going to jump out of his chest. The second Charlotte had started talking to him and pretending he was her mother he'd clearly known something was wrong. But when he'd heard her scream he'd thought he might lose ten years of his life. He'd been downtown already so getting here had taken ten minutes. Even if they'd felt like an entire lifetime.

The police had already sectioned off the alley where a dead body lay. They weren't letting either him or Charlotte near it and that was fine with both of them. She was sitting a foot away from him on a bench in front of a historic hotel that had shut down their front entrance for the time being. She held Reece in her arms. He was wide awake and looking around in curiosity as he sucked on his pacifier, but thankfully he was too young to understand what was going on. He was too young to do much of anything other than eat and sleep. A small blessing.

"Sir, we just need to ask her a few more questions." The uniformed police officer was just doing her job. The petite Hispanic woman had her hair pulled back into a tight bun and her expression was soft when she glanced at Charlotte. "I have a young daughter myself so I can imagine how stressful this is for her, but we need to take her down to the station to give a full report and talk to a sketch artist."

Kell gritted his teeth, hating that she'd have to go down there and hating more the fact that she'd witnessed a murder and had come close to losing her own life if that scumbag had gotten any closer. He couldn't know for sure, but the man had just killed someone in an alley and Kell seriously doubted he'd have let Charlotte live if he suspected she'd seen him.

His heart was still working overtime as he tried to convince himself that the two people who meant more to him than anything were okay. "And I understand that, we're just waiting on..." He trailed off, relief flooding him as he spotted Harrison Caldwell, one of the owners of Red Stone Security, striding down the sidewalk. He had Anthony Carlson, a member of Miami PD's SWAT team, with him. Hell yeah. Kell had known he would need reinforcements when Charlotte had whispered the most terrifying statement in his ear. *"A cop was involved in this."* Miami had a good department, but there was no way in hell he was letting anything get covered up or putting Charlotte in harm's way because of a leak. She was only talking to a select few about what she'd seen. As well-meaning as this officer seemed, she was just a beat cop and he needed someone higher up the chain. Someone they could trust.

"Delgado, good to see you, but I've got it from here," Carlson said as he stopped in between them. He was wearing street clothes, but the woman clearly knew who he was.

She flipped her notepad shut. "You sure? A detective will be on scene in a few minutes."

Carlson nodded, his dark eyes serious. He waited until the woman was out of earshot before turning to look at Kell. Harrison stood a few feet away, hovering next to Charlotte and Reece. When he asked to hold Kell's baby Kell was surprised, but kept his focus on Carlson.

The man scrubbed a hand over his face, sighing. "Is she sure there was a cop involved in this?"

Kell hadn't had a chance to talk to her in private so he only knew what little she'd relayed to the police and that one thing she'd told him. Nodding, he looked to Charlotte, whose eyes were wide and face pale as she glanced back and forth between him and Carlson.

"Honey," he said softly, "This is Anthony Carlson and you can trust him. We're going to have to go down to the station and you'll have to talk to a sketch artist, but you and Reece are going to be safe."

Even though he was way too young to understand anything, Reece made a gurgling sound at his name and grabbed Harrison's nose. Kell frowned at his boss, not liking how high he was holding Reece on his shoulder.

Charlotte's voice pulled his attention away. "If you trust him, I trust..." She trailed off, her face paling even more as she focused on something across the street. "That's him, that's the guy who was with the blond man who stabbed that poor man in the alley." She wrapped her arms around her middle as she started to shake.

A dark-haired man wearing jeans and a bomber jacket was talking to a uniformed officer who had been speaking to one of the people who'd witnessed Charlotte screaming and running for her life. Kell wrapped his arm around her shoulders, pulling her tight. She instantly leaned in to him, her shaking worsening.

"That fucker," Carlson cursed. "You're absolutely sure that's him?"

"He was two feet away from me. I'm sure," she rasped out, her voice trembling. Hell, no wonder. Kell was just impressed she'd managed to keep it together so long. Her smart thinking had saved her and Reece.

As if he knew he was being talked about, the man looked over at them. He made eye contact with Charlotte, his expression deadly. That was when Carlson took off at a full run across the street. The cops had completely sectioned off this block so the road was clear.

The man's gaze widened for a brief moment before he turned and sprinted in the other direction. He cut through the park disappearing behind a cluster of trees, but Carlson was gaining speed. The man moved like a trained runner.

"Holy crap," Charlotte murmured.

A few of the other officers were looking around in confusion at first. The uniformed woman who'd spoken to Charlotte earlier was the first to join in the pursuit, but other officers quickly followed.

"What are we supposed to do?" she asked.

Harrison answered before Kell could. "Just wait." They both turned to look at him and he continued. "Carlson will catch him and if he doesn't, that guy will be found soon. He wouldn't have run if he wasn't guilty. Probably didn't realize there was a witness until he showed up. My guess is after him and his partner murdered the man in the alley, they went dark." He shrugged as he spoke. "Don't worry. Miami PD won't put up with dirty cops. Whoever he is, he's going down."

Kell figured Harrison was right about the two men going dark. After killing someone, they wouldn't want any communication for a while. Not until the heat blew over. But there was still someone else out there. Someone else who'd seen Charlotte's face and had been close enough to harm Reece. Their innocent son. As if he read his expression and need to keep Reece close, Harrison handed him to Kell then motioned for Charlotte to sit back down. She practically collapsed on the bench, but instantly held out her arms for Reece. Though Kell wanted to hold his son he also understood her need. Handing him to her, Kell sat next to them and put an arm around her shoulders and pulled her close. He couldn't believe any of this was happening, but he was damn glad to be in their lives. No matter what happened, he would protect his own.

* * *

"The dead guy is part of a Mexican *cartel?*" Charlotte kept repeating everything Kell was relaying to her in question form but she couldn't stop it. Life had just gotten a whole lot scarier.

"No, he has an *association* with them," he said quietly. He sat on the opposite end of his couch, giving her a little distance as she tried to digest everything. She hadn't had to ask either; he seemed to read her very well and understood her need for space. After spending hours at the police station they were back at Kell's and Reece was sound asleep. Harrison had been calling with updates and Kell had just hung up with him only to give her more horrific news.

"What does that mean?"

"He's either done low level work for them or he's related either by blood or through business to someone in the cartel. Either way, this makes his killer a target, not you."

"How do we know the blond man who killed him isn't part of the cartel?" The thought made her entire body turn cold in fear.

"Carlson doesn't think he is. Your description and sketch match someone the guys from vice have been watching and *that* guy is in bed with one of their competitors."

They'd wanted her to look at pictures of criminals but Reece had been fussy and she'd been ready to get the hell out of there after talking to the sketch artist. Clearly they'd matched her picture up with someone. "So they've found him?"

Kell shook his head, his expression dark. "No, he's fallen off the face of the earth."

"What's his name?" She knew it wouldn't matter, but she wanted to put a name with that terrifying face. The one that had promised her certain death.

"His real name is Cecil Talley but apparently his street name is Ice Man."

Despite the entire horrific situation, Charlotte laughed under her breath at how stupid that sounded. Before she could ask another question, Kell answered one she'd been wondering about.

"And he's had suspected dealings with Reed West." The cop she'd seen that afternoon.

"So they killed someone with an 'association' with a freaking cartel and West isn't talking," she muttered to herself. Just great. Reed West was refusing to talk until he had a lawyer present and his lawyer wouldn't be in town until early tomorrow morning.

Even though there was nothing she could do about it, she felt as if she was in a state of limbo wondering and waiting what would happen next. If this thing ever went to trial she would have to testify and that brought on a whole other mess of fears.

"Come here." Kell's voice was low as he held out an arm.

Charlotte wanted to resist but right now she didn't have it in her as she scooted down and laid her head on his shoulder. It had been a long day and Kell had been there for her every step of the way, bringing in men he trusted, taking care of Reece when she couldn't. The man was a rock. She'd been on her own for what felt like forever and she was just getting the hang of this motherhood thing. She didn't want to get used to leaning on anyone if it wasn't going to last.

Not even Kell, who was not only walking, talking sex appeal, but a damn fine man. He'd totally stepped up when she told him about Reece, not even questioning his paternity. That meant more to her than she could ever express. But if she got used to all this support it would be that much harder to move out on her own in a few months.

His hold around her shoulders tightened as he placed his chin on top of her head. She inhaled, breathing in that masculine scent of his that had always driven her a little wild. Sliding a hand over his chest and around him, she savored the feel of all that hard muscle. It was hard not to remember what he'd looked like naked as he'd taken her hard and fast up against the hallway wall on the way to her bedroom a year ago. Then he'd taken her gentle and slow when they'd finally made it to her bed.

"You hungry?" he murmured.

Not for food. The thought took her by surprise, but it was true. The longer she was around him, the more that insistent attraction between them flared brighter. She should be too worried about the crisis hanging over her head to focus on anything else, but with Kell so near it was easy to let him distract her. She shook her head. "No."

The television was off, but he'd turned music on low earlier when she'd been giving Reece a bath. He'd even lit a few candles, which she didn't want to find sweet, but damn it, the man was getting under her skin. There was a dim lamp on in the corner of his living room. The atmosphere could be sensual if she let it. She hated that she wanted to. Instead of enjoying his embrace and thinking about what it would be like to have a repeat of that kiss yesterday, she should be heading to her room. "Thanks for being so supportive today," she finally murmured, feeling the need to say something.

He snorted softly. "You don't ever have to thank me for that."

"I know, it's just...I'd forgotten what that was like." When she'd first married Andrew things had been great between them. Hindsight was always easy, but she'd gotten married way too young. Now it was so clear to her. At twenty she hadn't even figured out who she was and what she wanted out of life. But she'd been smitten with the sexy FBI agent six years older than her. He'd been incredibly focused, loving, and now she realized that he'd loved how much she'd looked up to him. The first couple years of their marriage she'd been finishing up with college and their marriage had been easy. Once she'd started teaching full time, getting settled into her career and basically growing up a little more, the fractures in their marriage had started. Slowly at first, but now she could see how they'd both pulled away from each other. She hadn't needed him as much and he'd started to resent it.

Kell went impossibly still for a moment, then shifted against the couch. "How long were you guys having problems before he died?"

Surprised he'd asked, she said, "A few years." Sad considering they'd only been married for five before he died.

"I'm sorry." His quiet spoken words were sincere.

"Thanks. He wasn't a bad guy, even with the cheating. We just grew apart and for that, I'm sad, but I fell out of love with him years ago." The thought of leaving, of admitting that her marriage was a failure had been the most terrifying thing of all. No one in her family divorced. Now she wished she'd been braver, but if she had been, it was possible she might not have Reece. Who knew what path her life could have taken?

Kell grunted. "Cheating on you makes him a dick in my opinion."

Smiling at the annoyance in his voice, she looked up at Kell and into those pale, mesmerizing eyes. "I'm not making excuses for him, just stating a fact."

He didn't respond, but his gaze trailed to her lips with an intense focus before his eyes met hers. She could see what he wanted because she wanted the same thing. Leaning into a kiss would be so easy and after the day she'd had, she didn't want to be a coward and pull back from this. Before she could contemplate the ramifications of kissing him, he closed the short distance between them.

Unlike the intense kiss against her car yesterday, this one was soft and gentle. One of his hands slid into her hair as he cupped the back of her head. While the kiss was unhurried, his hold was firm, as if he was afraid she might bolt at any second. The thought crossed her mind but as his tongue swept against hers in erotic little strokes, she knew she wasn't walking away from this. Not now.

When he groaned into her mouth, she pulled back a fraction. He let out a frustrated sound until he realized what she was doing. Moving quickly, she straddled him. She wasn't ready to take things to a level beyond kissing at the moment, but she wanted to feel his body against hers. And feel it she did. He let out a strangled sound as she slid over his erection and settled in place. "Kissing only right now." She needed to let him know where she was emotionally.

Kell's smile was slow and seductive. "I could kiss you all night," he whispered back.

She was already growing damp and her nipples had tightened to hard points as she slid farther down his hard length. While she might not be ready for anything else tonight, she savored the feel of him, remembering how he'd felt as he'd pumped into her slick body over and over. They'd had sex so many times, that night was branded into her mind.

As she leaned toward his mouth, the sound of breaking glass and a car alarm blaring made them both freeze. The sound was too close to be anything other than her car, especially since his vehicle was in the garage. Before she could blink, he shifted her off him and withdrew a gun from behind his back.

Her eyes widened in shock. She knew he had multiple weapons in the house, but she hadn't realized he was carrying one on his person. "Go check on Reece." His softly spoken words were an order.

Normally that tone would irritate her, but they both wanted their son safe. Forcing down the panic rising inside her, she hurried to her son's room. Once she found him quietly sleeping, she allowed a sliver of relief to slide into her veins, but not much more. She tried to remain calm and unhurried as she gently lifted him from his bassinet. If they had to run, she wanted to be ready to leave.

When Kell found her minutes later, his expression was grim. "Your tires have been slashed and one of your windows broken. I've called the police and Harrison. I'd already asked him to have someone watch our place for the night, but they weren't supposed to show up until later. He's sending someone now."

Any relief she'd had evaporated. She looked at her sleeping son, then Kell and tried to quell the nervous tremor in her voice. "Do you think this has anything to do with today?"

He frowned, his pale eyes seeming to grow darker. "It's a real possibility."

CHAPTER SEVEN

Kell shut the door behind the police officers. They'd been cordial, but there was very little they could do other than take a report at this point. Slashed tires and a broken window didn't exactly scream cartel attack—they favored burning tires thrown on the front lawn or bullets through the home as a warning. And it didn't seem like something that murdering bastard Cecil Talley would do either. He'd heard more from Carlson and according to him, Talley was suspected of half a dozen murders—all of them committed with a blade. He wasn't known for intimidation tactics, he just killed without any fanfare. Not to mention Kell couldn't see how anyone could have figured out where Charlotte was staying because she hadn't listed his address on her police report and he'd made damn sure they weren't followed home.

When he went to Reece's room and found it empty, his heart rate jumped up a notch. The bassinet wasn't in there. Maybe Charlotte had moved him to her room. But they weren't in her room either. As he stepped back out into the hall, panic hadn't had a chance to set in when she stepped from the room at the end of the hall.

His room.

She gave him a tentative smile and wrapped her arms around herself as he strode toward her. She'd changed into a black long-sleeved pajama set with white hearts all over it. "Hey, I moved Reece in here and I was hoping I could stay with you tonight. *Just* to sleep. After what happened I'm not afraid to admit I'm freaked out right now. I want both of us close to you."

Definitely not the circumstances he'd wanted to get her into bed again, but he wasn't going to complain. "You can move into my bed permanently." Might as well get the truth out there. He'd made himself clear, but knowing what she'd had to go through because of her dead husband—unlike her, Kell wasn't cutting Andrew any slack for the way he'd treated her—he had no problem reaffirming his intent.

Her face flushed pink as her lips pulled into a thin line. "I know I kissed you, but—"

"Just leave it." He didn't want to hear how it was a mistake. Not when his chest constricted and he found it hard to freaking breathe when he was around her. He might know that she didn't feel the same as him, but he didn't need it spelled out.

"You don't even know what I was going to say."

"I can guess."

Rolling her eyes, she let her hands drop. "Fine, I'm tired and I know you must be too. Did the police say anything else?"

He shook his head. When Reece had started crying she'd left to feed him so Kell had wrapped things up with the police. "No, but someone from Red Stone is coming over to watch the house. With my security system no one is getting in here without the cops being alerted, but I want men I've worked with out there." Because he knew they were all highly trained, with most of them having former military experience.

She let out a shaky breath of relief and taking him completely by surprise, she crossed the few feet between them and wrapped her arms around his waist, laying her head on his chest. "I can't believe any of this is happening...I bet you're sorry you invited Reece and me to live with you now," she said half-jokingly.

"Never," he murmured against her hair, inhaling that sweet jasmine scent.

Everything about her was intoxicating. When she shifted against him, he nearly groaned at the feel of her breasts pressing into him, of her lush body lined up with his. What he wouldn't give to run his hands down to her ass and hoist her up so that she wrapped her legs around him. The memories of their one night together wouldn't leave him alone. Being under the same roof was just making them more vivid. But she clearly wasn't ready for more just yet. It was a good thing he was patient.

* * *

Charlotte opened her eyes as the warmth of the sun spread over her face. Stretching her arms above her head, she savored the quiet then realized just how silent the room was. She shoved the comforter off her and sat up. Reece wasn't in his bassinet and Kell wasn't on his side of the bed.

After a brief moment of panic it registered that he'd clearly let her sleep in. Something she hadn't been able to do the last three months. The rich scent of coffee filled the air so she washed her face, brushed her teeth and went in search of Kell and Reece.

She heard the soft murmur of male voices as she neared the kitchen, but couldn't make out actual words. As she stepped into the bright room she froze when she saw Kell and two other men. Harrison Caldwell was one of them. He was nice and polite, but he had a dark edge to him that was unnerving. The other man she recognized from the Garcia's party the other night. With dark skin and pale blue eyes that almost seemed to glow in contrast, he had a GQ quality to him. He might look like a pretty boy but he had that same military bearing to him that Kell did. After being married to a military/law enforcement guy she was pretty good at picking them out and this guy definitely had military experience too.

Her gaze immediately strayed to Kell who was leaning against the counter and holding a cooing Reece in his arms. Before she could ask what was going on, Kell nodded at the two men sitting at the island center. "You remember Harrison and this is Vincent. He works for Red Stone and we were in the Teams together."

A former SEAL too. So she'd been right. She smiled politely at them. "I remember you from the party."

At that, the newcomer smiled almost cheekily. "You remember me?"

Yeah because she'd caught him staring at her butt on more than one occasion. At Kell's annoyed growl, she bit back a smile and headed for the full pot of coffee. "You might as well tell me what's going on. I know you all aren't here for a social call." Her voice sounded a lot calmer than she felt but that was probably because she didn't have any caffeine in her body. She was still a little too tired to get worked up about anything yet.

"Why don't you have a seat?" Kell murmured.

Shooting him an annoyed look as she snagged one of the mugs he'd laid out, she shook her head and dropped a kiss on Reece's forehead. "I'm okay. What's going on?" She didn't need to be coddled—she wanted to know what was going on.

"Reed West is dead," Harrison said quietly.

Mug in hand, Charlotte leaned against the counter so that she was touching Kell. She let the feel of him ground her. "The cop? How?" He was supposed to have been in jail, but protected from the general population. That was what Kell had told her.

"Poison." Kell bit the word out. "He was in isolation but someone got to him."

"What does this mean for me? Do they know who killed him? It's got to be related to yesterday, right?" Coffee forgotten, questions flew out of her mouth as she gripped the counter for support. For a moment all she could do was focus on Reece, thankful he was okay. She wanted to hold him but was too shaky.

Kell seemed to sense that. "I've got him," he murmured and she wanted to bury her face in his neck and absorb all that strength. With his free hand, he rubbed the small of her back as she turned to face the other two.

Vincent was quiet and she figured he was just there in a backup capacity when Harrison spoke. "At this point, there are only guesses as to why he was killed, but there are only two scenarios that truly work."

"Okay." She just prayed that either of them were good for their safety.

"West was a dirty cop who was involved with the murder of a man named Mateo Diaz. Mateo's brother is an enforcer for the Mexican cartel based in Miami so either someone from the cartel—or his brother personally—got to West. If that's what happened, it's good for you."

"Uh, why?"

He shrugged. "Multiple reasons. If the cartel is cleaning up then they'll go after the other man involved in the murder. It means Talley won't be a threat to you anymore and he's too low in the hierarchy of his gang for anyone to give a crap about."

That left one other option, and from the way Kell stilled she knew she was going to hate whatever Harrison had to say next.

"If Talley's gang got to West—which at this point the gang unit seriously doubts—then you might be a target. You're the only other person who can identify Talley as Diaz's murderer."

She took a steadying breath. "Why does the gang unit doubt his gang is involved?"

"First, Talley has only recently made a connection with the 19th Street Gang. Hell, killing Diaz was probably part of his initiation, but he could still be on a probationary period with them. Second, they're small potatoes. Of the two hundred plus gangs in south Florida they don't have the kind of pull to poison a prisoner in private holding."

Charlotte had no idea what to think or feel other than be terrified. "But if the 19th Street Gang is involved and they're the ones behind the killing, they could come after me next?" And they wouldn't care who got in the way. The thought of putting Reece or Kell in harm's way made nausea swell inside her. Why couldn't she have ignored those cries of distress from that alley? She inwardly groaned. No matter what, she would have checked it out and she couldn't go back and change the past anyway.

"Even if the 19th Street Gang isn't involved, Talley is still out there and you're still a witness," Kell said, still frowning.

"So what am I supposed to do?"

Before he could respond, Harrison cleared his throat. "We're assuming you don't want to go to your parents' because it's the first place anyone with half a brain would look for you."

She nodded, not because of his reason but because she would never put her family in danger.

"We can either put you in a temporary safe house with guards or you can stay with my brother Porter and his wife. They live in one of the safest high rises in the city. It's impossible to penetrate and they're expecting a baby so you wouldn't need to move any of Reece's stuff. He can sleep in their nursery."

Her jaw tightened. "You want me to possibly put a pregnant woman in harm's way?"

Kell let out a long breath, drawing her attention to him. Reece had dozed again but she knew he'd be hungry soon. "You have no association with either of them and we'll make damn sure you're not followed there. It's secure and you won't be dealing with a bunch of armed guards living with you, though there will be guards outside their place. Lizzy is six months along now and doing a lot of her work from home."

Charlotte blinked in confusion as she glanced at Harrison. "Lizzy...Caldwell is your brother's wife. I didn't even put the names together until now. Her parents are acquaintances with mine. I met her at the Garcia party. You're absolutely sure they're okay with this?"

Harrison nodded so she glanced at Kell. "What do you think?"

"Until we locate Talley I don't want you or Reece to be an easy target. I can't think of one possible way anyone would find you at Porter's place. We'll be giving you a company cell phone so even if someone attempts to track your cell, they won't be able to." His expression was blank so she couldn't tell what he was thinking or how he felt about being separated from her.

When Reece's eyes opened and he started fussing she immediately took him, cuddling him close to her chest. He calmed immediately, but she glanced at the two other men then Kell. "Can we talk privately?" she whispered.

He nodded then excused them.

In the privacy of his bedroom she started feeding Reece, and tried to ignore the way Kell's gaze strayed to her breasts. "How long is this supposed to go on? Me and Reece hiding?"

He sat on the edge of the bed. "I don't know. Red Stone has resources the police don't and Harrison is very protective of his employees. If he's still in the city, we're going to find Cecil Talley and turn him over to the police."

"I'm not a Red Stone employee." Or even family to one of them.

"You're mine," Kell practically growled.

Okay, then. She swallowed hard before asking her next question. "What about you? Will I be able to see you while I'm staying there?" The thought of uprooting again especially after starting to get settled and comfortable with Kell was unnerving. It stunned her how much the thought of leaving him hurt.

He shook his head, his expression dark. "We can talk on the phone, but I don't want to inadvertently lead someone to you guys. Keeping you and Reece safe is more important."

"So how long do you think we'll be there?" Because they were going. She might not want to uproot again, but she would do it. Her baby's safety was all that mattered.

"A couple weeks at the most."

"I'm going to miss you." The words were out before she could stop herself, but they were true.

Kell looked surprised, but that quickly gave way to a purely male, satisfied smile. "I'm going to miss you too. But it won't be long, I promise."

As Reece finished feeding, she closed her top and didn't try to stop him when Kell gently picked him up and placed him in the bassinet. The kid slept more than he was awake. Charlotte was just thankful that if something insane like all this had to happen, it was happening when he was too young to understand what was going on or to remember.

"I guess I should start packing."

Kell nodded, but knelt in front of her. With his height, they were practically eye level. Instinctively she spread her legs so he could move in closer. Wordlessly, he leaned forward, his mouth capturing hers as his hand slid behind her head in that dominating grip she loved. Before she'd even gotten fully into the kiss she found herself flat on her back and Kell stretched out on top of her. He definitely didn't hesitate in going for what he wanted.

Since he'd shut the door behind them she wasn't worried about anyone walking in without knocking.

As Kell's tongue stroked hers, his lips teasing and gentle, she lightly moaned and arched into him. The thought of not being able to see him after just walking back into his life shook her to her core. He gave her a sense of security in a way that was almost terrifying because he also threatened the quiet life she'd started rebuilding for herself. She'd never imagined he'd want her to move in or even physically still want her so much. When he suddenly paused, his hand barely grazing her breast, her eyes flew open.

"What's wrong?" she whispered, not wanting to break the quiet spell of the room.

Looking nervous, Kell glanced at the bassinet on the other side of the room then back at her.

She tried to fight a smile and lost. "You're worried about Reece?"

Slowly Kell nodded, his expression torn between lust and worry.

Unable to stop herself, she let out a low laugh. He could hold his head up when sitting, though it still bobbed around, but he was too young to sit up on his own or realize what was going on. "He can't lift his head up far enough to see us and he's way too young to understand what's going on even if he was awake."

"You're sure?"

"I've read every baby book out there, but if you want to stop—"

He silenced her with another kiss. Okay, he didn't want to stop either. She wasn't sure what she wanted right now, but the only thing she knew for sure was that she wanted Kell's hands on her. Even if she was terrified of the thought of him seeing her naked. Her body had changed since the last time he'd seen her. Her hips were a little wider and she was softer.

When he reached between them and slowly began unbuttoning her top she frantically reached for his hands, stilling him.

He lifted up, his pale eyes worried. "What's wrong?"

"Nothing, it's just...I look different than I used to before I had Reece." What if he didn't want her anymore? What if he decided that—

"You actually think I give a shit about that?"

The heat she saw in his gaze killed most of her fears. She slowly shook her head, but didn't trust herself enough to speak.

With his gaze on her, he continued unbuttoning the black and white pajama top until she was splayed out for him. As his eyes zeroed in on her breasts, the rest of her fear dissolved. He definitely wanted her. She could see it in every harsh line of his features.

"Are your breasts sore?" The thoughtful question once again took her by surprise, but by now she figured she should be used to it.

She nodded. "They're tender."

"We can work around that." He bent his head to her breast but instead of taking her nipple in his mouth like she'd expected he gently kissed the underside of her mounds, licking and raking his teeth over the soft flesh.

He teased her everywhere except her nipples, which were a little too tender at the moment.

It floored her how he seemed to read her moods and needs.

When he began a slow path down her stomach, her lower abdomen muscles clenched in anticipation. As he reached her C-section scar and kissed along the fading incision mark, she knew what was coming. The dampness between her thighs grew, making her feel slightly embarrassed that she was this turned on.

He hadn't even taken his clothes off yet. "Shirt off," she demanded.

Kell raised his head in surprise at her command, but without question grasped the edge of his T-shirt and peeled it off. She sucked in a breath as her gaze trailed up his washboard stomach to the hard lines of his chest. As she reached his shoulders she blushed furiously. She'd clutched on to them as he'd pounded into her against a wall. Then she'd thrown her legs over them as he'd gone down on her at the end of her bed.

"Your eyes are so expressive," he murmured before grasping the top of her pajama pants. He hooked his fingers around her panties and tugged them off at the same time. She still had her shirt on even if it was unbuttoned, yet she felt completely naked. Exposed to him. After the past few days her nerves were raw and shot to hell. She needed this. They both did.

She went to sit up and reach for the top of his pants, but he shook his head. "Lay back. Now."

The hard command in his voice had her nipples tightening and her inner walls clenching with need. His palms pressed against her knees, spreading her legs wider as he dipped his head between her thighs.

"I've dreamed about this," he murmured before his tongue swiped up her slit.

She jerked against the sheets and bit back a moan. Considering they had people waiting for them in the kitchen and a sleeping baby nearby, she knew she needed to be quiet.

His tongue slowly dipped inside her, teasing and flicking before he ran it back up to her clit. Unable to stop herself she grabbed his head, threading her fingers through his dark hair. A shudder rippled through her when his tongue circled her clit, enflaming the sensitive bundle of nerves.

"Kell," she moaned his name, wanting to shout it. He was the last man she'd been with so her body was primed and tense with so much need. She'd been fantasizing about a repeat of what they'd shared for the last year.

He smiled against her wet flesh. "You've got to stay quiet," he whispered

With her free hand she fisted the sheet beneath her. Her fingers dug into the material as he began his assault anew, licking and teasing until she was shaking with the need to cry out, to climax. She was so damn close to the edge and all she wanted to do was come, to feel his thick length pushing deep inside her.

When he quickly pushed one, then two fingers inside her she was lost. He was gentle, watching her for feedback as he began stroking her. The orgasm that punched through her was sharp, slapping all her nerve endings with a startling intensity she hadn't expected. Her legs tightened around his head but he didn't seem to care as he pumped his fingers in and out of her in a steady rhythm, his tongue never letting up from her clit.

As her climax began to ebb he lightly pressed his teeth around her little nub, sending another one shooting through her. Her back arched off the bed, her inner walls clenching furiously around his fingers as she bathed him in her cream until she collapsed against the sheets unable to move.

An instant later he climbed up her body and feathered kisses along her jaw and lips. She could taste herself on him and even though she was spent, she reached for the top of his pants, wanting to see all of him. But he quickly stopped her with a strong grip on her wrists.

"Why are you stopping me?" Hurt lanced through her at the rejection.

He must have read her expression because he shook his head. "It's not because I don't want this. I do, more than anything. But when I take you again it's going to be for hours and it's not going to happen with people a few rooms over and our baby in the room. I'm going to fuck you so long that you scream my name from the pleasure of it. Then I'm going to do it again."

Still unsteady, she sat up, but wrapped her hands around him, lacing her fingers together behind his neck. "Then why..." she trailed off, not needing to finish. Why had he done this if he wouldn't let her return the favor?

"I want you to think about this while we're separated. I want you to remember how good things are between us." His voice was almost guttural, needy as he kissed her again.

She had no doubt that she'd remember this because she still hadn't forgotten their last time together. Kell had branded her their first and only night together in a way that still stunned her. It was almost like he could read her mind. Or maybe he just paid attention. He was so possessive in the bedroom, so demanding and yet so tender and gentle. Unlike her deceased husband, Kell made her feel wanted in a way that was indescribable. When he looked at her, she knew he was hungry for her. And she definitely reciprocated.

Right now the last thing in the world she wanted to do was leave Kell. To keep her son and him safe she'd do anything, but it didn't mean she liked it. Especially not when she was starting to realize that they might have a chance at a real relationship.

CHAPTER EIGHT

Cecil Talley pulled his cap lower on his head as he strode down the sidewalk of the lower middle-class neighborhood he used to call home. His grandmother still lived there, but he didn't see her much anymore. Not with his lifestyle. She'd done the best she could to raise him once his mother had split and he couldn't bring any heat on her. She didn't deserve it.

He'd driven by a few times in the past couple days and hadn't seen any cops or worse, cartel members loitering around. Cecil still couldn't believe that cop West was dead. They'd planned to kill Mateo Diaz and make it look like a robbery gone wrong—then later the 19th Street Gang would take credit for it. Cecil hadn't worked with West before, but the man accepted bribes from certain gangs in the area and he occasionally looked the other way. The cop had just been with him to make sure the job got done right—as if Cecil needed a fucking babysitter. But then that witness had fucked everything up. They'd been careful too, picking a deserted alley, the right time of day, everything.

And that bitch had come out of nowhere. Worse, West had been murdered in *prison*. Where he should have been protected. Talley knew what that meant. The cartel had gotten to him. And now the 19th Street Gang had hung *him* out to dry. Killing Mateo was supposed to have brought Mateo's brother, Renaldo, out of hiding. Then the gang was going to kill him and make a name for themselves. Mateo wasn't involved with the cartel. He'd been in hospitality of all things, but as Renaldo's brother he'd been considered to have an 'association' with them. So it had been well known that he was off limits. But the 19th Street boys had decided to make a move against him anyway—using Cecil to do the dirty work.

Instead, with the cop dead, the guys he thought were his friends had abandoned him. His nerves were shot by trying to lay low and he was dying for a cigarette but he hadn't wanted to show up here stinking. His grandma hated it when he smoked. Hell, he hated that he even had to come here, but before getting out of town he had to pick up his stash from his grandmothers and kill the witness. While he didn't like to kill women, he'd do it. At this point he was just trying to survive and he couldn't take the risk that he left town with someone out there who'd seen him commit murder. It would always be hanging over his head since there was no statute of limitations on murder in Florida.

It was too much to hope that killing her might elimi-nate his other, bigger problem: Renaldo Diaz. The scary-ass enforcer for the growing cartel probably knew who he was if West had talked in prison—but there was a slim chance West had kept his mouth shut and Diaz didn't know of his involvement. Of course none of that would matter if the woman had been able to identify him to the police because sooner or later that information would find its way to Renaldo. Either way, the woman had to die.

Instead of walking up to his grandmother's front door, he cut through her next door neighbor's yard and hopped the fence into the backyard. The drunk who lived there didn't get up until at least noon and it was only seven in the morning. He jumped the fence into his grandma's backyard and tried to sneak in through the back door, but she was in the kitchen cooking. With her back to him, she shook her dark head. "Sit and eat before you hightail out of here again." Though her words were flippant, he heard the hurt there and it sliced through him.

He hated hurting her but if he hung out here more often she'd be a target. Now she was just some old lady he'd lived with for a few years. At least that was how his associates viewed her. Crossing the distance over the newly tiled floor—which he'd paid for by selling drugs—he dropped a kiss on the top of her head. At five feet flat she was an entire foot shorter than him. She was only in her fifties but his mom had had him young. Despite having had a bitch for a daughter and cleaning up Cecil's mom's messes for years, his grandmother looked like she was in her forties. At least genetics had been kind to her. "What're you cooking?"

She looked up at him and smiled, the lines around her mouth crinkling. "Fried eggs, sausage and grits, your favorite."

It was his favorite but she couldn't have known he was coming. Which meant she probably cooked this every morning in the hopes that he'd show up. Yeah, he was an asshole.

"Police were here yesterday," she continued as she pulled out one of the new plates from the set he'd bought her last month.

Turning away so he wouldn't have to see her expression, he opened the fridge and pretended to look for something. "Yeah? What'd they want?"

"Looking for you. Told 'em I haven't seen you in months—which is the truth."

Pulling out a carton of milk, he faced her. "You know why I can't hang around here, grandma."

Her dark eyes narrowed and he felt like the teenage boy she'd tried scolding hundreds of times. While he'd always been respectful since she was the only person who'd ever given a damn about him, he'd never listened. But he'd gotten better about lying over the years. Now it was useless to lie. Especially if he wouldn't see her for a while.

"If the cops come back, tell them the truth, that I stopped by but I told you I'd be leaving town for a while."

She turned to the stove again, her back ramrod straight. "You're leaving?"

He leaned against the counter next to her, forcing her to look at him. "I've got to. I...got into some trouble and if I stick around I'll bring too much heat on me and you. The last thing I ever want to do is hurt you, grandma."

Her jaw clenched and though she wouldn't look directly at him he saw unshed tears glistening in her eyes as she stared at the popping frying pan. "I appreciate all the stuff you've done around the house for me, but I don't need it. I just need you safe and in my life."

"I know." With his throat tight, he pushed away and went to sit at the table. Didn't matter what either of them wanted. Life had taught him that early on.

He steeled himself against the coming week. First he needed to find the witness and eliminate her, then he'd figure out where the hell to head after that. Maybe Chicago. He had some buddies from the old neighborhood who'd moved up there. The thought of dealing with snow was revolting but anything was better than the heat coming down on him here. Maybe he could move his grandma up there after a few years too. Yeah, that could work.

As he waited for her to finish cooking, one of his cell phones buzzed in his pocket. *5-0 asking about you to the boys. Stay away from the neighborhood.* Translation: the cops were questioning the 19th Street Gang about him and he better stay the hell way from them right now. So he was on his own. Ungrateful fucking bastards.

CHAPTER NINE

*K*ell scrubbed a hand over his face, feeling nervous as hell as he stood on Charlotte's front porch. He shouldn't be here. How many times had he told himself that he needed to stay the fuck away from her, that being around her was going to eventually slice up his heart?

But he couldn't stay away. The woman called to him on a primal level and he was like that proverbial moth to a flame. He knew he'd end up getting burned too. Pretty soon he'd go down in a ball of flames because of his own stupidity and need.

After their last phone call and the weird way she'd been acting, he had to stop by though. It had almost sounded like she was crying, which wasn't strange considering her circumstances, but he couldn't help but feel like something else was going on.

He rang the doorbell and tensed as he tried to prepare himself to see her again, to prepare himself for the slam of physical need he always experienced in her presence. Not that it would do any good.

A few moments later the door swung open. Wearing snug jeans and a breast-hugging plain black T-shirt that dipped right between her breasts, she looked good enough to eat. Her *face was pale, her dark eyes watery and she looked more an-gry than sad. She also appeared surprised to see him. "Hey."*

His tongue stuck to the roof of his mouth for a second. "Hey...I probably should have called, but you sounded upset during our last call so..." He shrugged as he trailed off, feeling awkward.

"No, it's fine." She stepped back, motioning with her hand for him to enter. "You want to come in?"

Always. *"Sure." He held up a small white paper bag with pink lettering on it. He'd decided to grab her some petit fours from her favorite bakery. "Brought you something."*

Her dark gaze landed on the bag, then traveled back to him and for the first time since he'd known her he saw lust in her gaze. Pure, raw need.

For him.

He wasn't imagining it either. He'd seen that look plenty of times from other women. Never from her though. What the hell was going on with her?

She swallowed hard and took the bag, a sad smile on her face. "You're always so damn thoughtful." For some reason the words sounded almost accusing.

She set the bag on the small table in the foyer, then leaned up on tiptoe and kissed him. And not on the cheek as she had a hundred times before. No, she kissed him straight on the mouth, her lips molding to his. Kell was so stunned he forgot how to breathe for a second. But only for a second.

Then he was on her, unable to leash the need he'd been carrying around for years. His hands flexed around her hips as she hoisted herself up and wrapped her legs around him. Taking him even more by surprise, she clawed at his shirt, desperate to get it off.

He backed her up against the nearest wall, needing a flat surface as he managed to shrug his shirt off.

Part of him wondered what the hell had brought this on, but he was too damn selfish to question why she'd made the decision to come to him now. He wanted her more than he wanted his next breath.

Grasping the hem of her shirt, he pulled it up her lean body to reveal full, round breasts. The simple black bra she wore was utilitarian but the way it pushed those mounds up for him...he fought a shudder and lost.

He'd been fantasizing about what the color of her nipples would be for so long. He didn't take her bra off, but pulled the straps down so that her breasts spilled free.

Pale, pink nipples.

Now he could stop guessing. When her fingers slid into his hair, clutching on to his head, he dipped lower, sucking one of her nipples into his mouth. Flicking it with his tongue, he shuddered when she let out a loud moan and arched deeper into his mouth.

She was every fantasy he'd ever had...

A pounding sound had Kell opening his eyes. Confused, he looked around and realized he must have dozed on his couch. Of course he had to dream about *that* night with Charlotte. That hadn't happened in forever...What the hell was that pounding?

His front door.

Pushing up, he glanced through the peephole before pulling the door open.

Vincent stood there in jeans, a sweater and holding a six-pack of beer. He lifted it up. "Figured you might want the company tonight."

It was his first night without Charlotte and Reece, and while he hadn't thought he would want to be around anyone, relief slid through him at the sight of his friend. He nodded. "Come on. I think there's a game on."

Turning on his flat screen, he collapsed on one end of the couch and Vincent handed him a beer. "You got any food?"

He nodded. "Help yourself to whatever's in the fridge."

After some rumbling around in the kitchen, Vincent returned a few minutes later with a bag of chips, a sandwich and a beer. He sat on the other end of the couch and began to devour his food.

As a football game played in the background Kell glanced at his cell phone on the end table next to his couch. Right now it was hard to concentrate on anything but Charlotte. He was relieved that she was able to stay with Lizzy and Porter, and after talking to her earlier tonight it was clear that she was getting along well with the other woman, but he wanted her here.

Under the same roof. Protected by him. Especially after that fucking dream. He rubbed his hand over his face as if that could erase the memories. That night had been intense, but the next morning...yeah, no need to go there.

"So what's up with you and Charlotte? Can't believe you moved her in here so fast." Vincent crumpled his napkin up and threw it on his empty plate.

"Why?"

"I knew you were hung up on someone when you moved here, but moving a readymade family in like that..." He trailed off, shrugging. "It's a big change, man. That's all I'm saying."

"She's all I've ever wanted and we have a son together." It was as simple as that. Now that he'd had her under his roof, even if it had only been for a few days, he knew he was never letting her go.

"You love her?"

"What do you think?" Kell hadn't said the words to Charlotte again since that night a year ago and he sure as hell wasn't saying it to Vincent before her.

"I almost got married once," Vincent said a few minutes later, his gaze straight ahead on the television, his jaw tight.

Kell's eyebrows rose. Vincent Hansen had almost been married? For as long as he'd known him the man had been more than a player. He was what their friend Lizzy called a man-whore. "Seriously?"

"Yep. After I got out of the Teams, right when I'd started working for Red Stone. I loved her too. Then one day she up and left without a single fucking word. She was just gone." Still not looking at him, Vincent cracked open another beer and downed half of it in seconds. "I like Charlotte, but...be careful."

Kell didn't respond, just sipped his own beer and stared blindly at the screen. How the hell could he be careful? She already owned him, even if she didn't know it yet.

* * *

Charlotte tugged her long-sleeved pink and white checkered pajama top on and went in search of Reece and Lizzy. Lizzy's husband was working late, but they had two guards outside the expensive high rise condo.

The tall, beautiful Hispanic woman had offered—well, insisted was more like it—to take Reece off her hands so Charlotte could shower. Since Reece had gone willingly to the other woman, Charlotte had taken advantage.

She found Lizzy on the long white couch in the living room with a laptop on her lap and Reece sleeping in the bassinet next to her. Drapes had been pulled to cover the high windows that in the morning would bathe the living room and kitchen in sunlight. Lizzy looked up and smiled. "He drank one of the bottles and just went to sleep. That kid can sure eat."

Charlotte smiled and sat on the loveseat on the other side of her sleeping son. "Tell me about it. He's in the ninetieth percentile for height right now so something tells me he'll be tall like Kell." All that could change over the next couple years but Reece was a mini version of his father.

Lizzy's dark eyes narrowed curiously at the mention of Kell. Without looking at her screen, she typed in a few commands, then shut the laptop, her gaze still on Charlotte. "What's up with you two?"

Charlotte shrugged, not even remotely sure how to answer. She was pretty sure she'd completely fallen for Kell and had no clue what the right move was, especially considering she couldn't even see him until this mess was settled. "Ah, I don't know."

"I'm totally being nosy so if I ask too many questions you don't want to answer you won't hurt my feelings if you tell me to shut up. That said—what made you decide to move in with him? I didn't even know Kell had a...anyone, until Porter told me you needed a place to hide out."

"Circumstances didn't really give me much of a choice." That was a vague enough answer and all she felt comfortable telling the other woman. "Not that I didn't want to." As soon as the words were out of her mouth she realized they were true.

No matter what she wanted to tell herself, she liked living with Kell. Liked being under the same roof as him even if the memory of their hot night together was driving her a little crazy. "Long story short, he deserves time with his son and my alcoholic sister moved back in with my parents. I was already looking for a place to move, but..." She trailed off, not wanting to get into the whole big thing with this woman no matter how nice she was.

Lizzy's lips pulled into a thin line for a moment then she smiled. "All right, I won't bother you with any more questions. Not until we get to know each other better...You want some hot tea?"

Charlotte nodded and turned Reece's bassinet toward her as the other woman got up. Answering a bunch of questions was the last thing she wanted right now but she could definitely do with the female companionship. After she'd gotten pregnant with Reece she'd lost a lot of friends back in DC. She figured some people had known about her husband's infidelities, but most people hadn't.

Or she assumed they hadn't considering that people she'd thought were friends had come down so hard on her about something that was none of their damn business anyway.

Sighing, she laid her head back on the loveseat, listening to the sound of the teapot whistle from the other room. Tomorrow was a new day and she just prayed that whoever was after her would be found soon so she could figure out the rest of her life. One that hopefully included Kell.

CHAPTER TEN

Two weeks later

"**M**onique, this is getting really old," Kell growled into the phone. Monique had been practically stalking him for the past two weeks, calling at all hours of the night and day. Hell, she'd even shown up at his house again a few times. Thank God Charlotte wasn't there. After what she'd been through with her ex, he didn't want her to think he actually wanted this woman around. The Red Stone Security guys thought Monique was fucking hilarious and a few single ones had told him to send her their way, but she was grating on his last nerve. With all the shit going on in his life and the fact that he hadn't been able to see Charlotte or Reece over the past two weeks, his temper was on a hair trigger.

"I think I heard someone breaking into my house though," she whispered, her voice teary.

For the brief time they'd dated she'd been cool, elegant and almost standoffish—until the last few days before he'd ended things. She'd started acting needy and...weird. "Then hang up and call the police. Stop calling and stop coming by my house or I'm filing a restraining order." Not waiting for a response, he hung up on her.

He thought he'd gotten rid of his problem by programming his smartphone to send any calls from her number directly to voicemail. Unfortunately she must have figured it out because she'd been calling from different numbers. Up until now he'd tried to be as polite as he could, but that clearly wasn't working so he had to try a different approach. Especially since Charlotte and Reece were coming home tonight.

The last two weeks without them had been hell. He'd spoken to Charlotte on the phone, but until he'd been absolutely sure the cartel wasn't a problem, he hadn't been willing to see her or Reece in person. Now Red Stone, the gang unit and vice from the police department had all confirmed that the cartel had no beef with Charlotte. She was nothing to them other than a confirmation of who'd been behind the killing of Mateo Diaz. If anything, they were probably grateful for her because without her statement to the police, they might not have ever known who'd killed Mateo. And Cecil Talley had fallen off the face of the earth. The cops had questioned his grandmother multiple times and the woman had told them she'd seen him last week and he'd said he was leaving town for good. Supposedly she didn't know why.

Kell wasn't certain if that was true, but the confidential informant that the gang unit had within the 19th Street Gang had reiterated that Talley was gone for good. So it seemed as if he wasn't a problem. With the cartel wanting his blood, he'd probably never come back to Miami.

Didn't mean Kell was letting his guard down though. He was bringing Charlotte and their son home, but for the next month he still planned to have a guard on them at all times. He also wanted to enroll her in self-defense classes.

Their safety meant everything.

At the sound of his doorbell, he tried to tamp down the need humming through him. Two weeks without Charlotte after feeling her climax around his fingers, after seeing that satisfied expression on her face, and he was going a little crazy. The past year without her had been difficult, but things were different now. She wasn't just coming off a bad marriage and hell, they had a son together. A son he desperately missed.

Even though he could sense her hesitancy to commit, Charlotte wanted him physically and he didn't mind playing up that connection. He'd use that against her every chance he got—in the shower, on the kitchen table, in the bedroom—anywhere she'd have him until she got the message that they were meant to be together.

After checking the peephole, he opened the door. Charlotte stood there holding a gurgling Reece against her chest. Even though Kell was pretty sure he was too young to recognize him, Reece made a loud giggling sound when he saw him and started waving his hands around with no coordination. Charlotte looked surprised but smiled and handed Reece to Kell as they stepped through the front door. He held his son close, savoring the feel of his small body against his. Reece stared at him with those big eyes, his expression so open and trusting it was hard to fathom that he'd helped create this tiny life. That Reece was a part of him.

Her guard for the drive over, Travis, who supposedly had piercings in places Kell didn't want to know about, stepped inside carrying two big bags. All business, he nodded once at Kell, letting him know the ride over had gone smoothly.

Charlotte wrapped her arms around herself, looking uncertain as she smiled tentatively at Kell. Was she nervous to be back here?

Before he could contemplate what that expression meant, she turned to Travis and gave him a genuine smile. The sight was like a punch to the gut. Why wasn't she looking at Kell like that? "Thanks for your company these past couple weeks. And please thank Noel for all the cookies she sent over. Once things settle down here I'm going to stop by her shop and meet her in person."

Travis smiled broadly and rubbed a hand over his head. "She'd like that." He tilted his head toward Reece. "Bring the little guy too, she loves babies."

Kell was more than thankful that Harrison had sent his best guys to guard Charlotte, but he didn't like the foreign feeling of jealousy welling up inside him. Travis was happily engaged and it was clear there was nothing romantic going on, but still, Charlotte was so damn re-laxed around the other guy. Why wasn't she like that with him? After the way they'd left things he'd expected her to jump him the minute she saw him. Okay, maybe not that soon, but he'd expected a warmer reception.

As soon as Travis was gone and it was the three of them, Charlotte gave him that tentative look again, as if she didn't know what to say. He started to say something when he got a whiff of an unpleasant smell coming from Reece. His son giggled and squirmed in his arms as if it was hilarious. "I'm gonna change his diaper but I'll help with your bags in a sec, okay?"

She nodded and he was sure he saw relief in her ex-pression as she said, "Okay."

Well, hell. Looked like they were back to square one.

* * *

Charlotte pulled out a bottle of wine from Kell's pan-try. She'd fed Reece before they arrived and she'd pumped enough for the rest of the night that she could savor a little wine. Right now she needed it. After two weeks without Kell she wasn't sure what her reception from him would be. The last time she'd seen him she'd still been basking in the glow of the orgasm he'd given her.

She almost felt like a teenager right now, worried and nervous being around him. The one night they'd spent together had been amazing, but it had been all about the sex. Now real life was in their faces. They had a baby, were living under the same roof, and man, the way Kell looked at her was enough to short-circuit her brain. She didn't want a relationship based on lust since that would fade. And she was terrified of the feelings he evoked in her because deep down, she knew it was more than lust.

As she popped the cork, she felt more than heard Kell. When she glanced over her shoulder she saw that he was alone. A thread of panic spooled through her. She'd been hoping he'd have Reece with him so she'd have that barrier. "Where's Reece?" Oh Lord, did her voice just shake?

"He's asleep." Kell leaned against the doorframe of the kitchen entry, watching her with those pale green eyes. He looked huge, imposing and made her feel unsettled.

Unnerved, she turned away and began to pour a glass. When some of the red liquid sloshed onto the counter she cursed her unsteadiness. Before she could grab a rag to clean it up, Kell was behind her, sliding his strong hands down her arms until his fingers covered hers. With his chest against her back she could feel the steady beat of his heart. She'd missed him and wanted nothing more than to lean back in his embrace.

Slowly, gently, he nipped her earlobe with his teeth, making her shiver in awareness. "Why are you acting nervous around me?" he murmured.

She let out a shaky laugh. "I'm not." Okay, that was lame. She didn't know why she was denying it.

"Hmmm." He didn't say anything more, just began a slow procession of kisses across the back of her neck. Lifting her hair as he moved, he kissed, licked, and gently raked his teeth over her sensitive skin until he reached her other earlobe. He pressed down just a little harder on that one. "Don't lie to me, Charlotte. What's going on?"

Her traitorous body flared to life with need as his deep voice rolled over her. When one of his hands slid up the front of her sweater, splaying across her stomach, she shuddered. Her abdomen muscles tightened in anticipation. How did he expect her to think when he was touching her?

"I've missed you." His mouth was right next to her ear, his breath warm against her skin.

"Me too." Probably too much. That scared the hell out of her. She didn't want to get used to having him in her life because she was afraid things wouldn't work out.

"The first time I saw you, you were wearing a bright red summer dress." His voice was a warm caress around her entire body. "When I saw you at the Garcia party, it reminded me of that first time."

He remembered what she'd been wearing the first time he'd seen her? She could barely remember her name right now. The sweetness of that totally stripped the rest of her meager defenses against him. He'd been so cool and remote the first time they'd met. "Oh."

His chuckle against her skin had a dark edge to it. His free hand joined his other one, grasping at the edge of her sweater. She started to turn, but he pressed his back against her, flattening her against the counter. "Don't move until I say."

Okay, then. She could definitely do that. The command in his voice sent a thrill through her. As he slowly began lifting her sweater up, she moved her arms when he told her to. Cool air rushed over her skin as he tossed her sweater onto the counter.

"I wanted to lift that summer dress up, bend you over the nearest surface and pound into you until neither of us could walk." His hands settled on her hips as his lips began a light trail of kisses down her spine.

Her inner walls clenched, needing to be filled by him. Breathing raggedly, she closed her eyes as his mouth moved down her back. It had been too long since she'd been with him and her body was tense with an unfulfilled hunger. The orgasm from a couple weeks ago had been wonderful, but she wanted more.

"When I realized you were taken I kept my distance. But then I found out how fucking sweet you were and couldn't stay away." His voice was raspy, unsteady. "I knew being friends with you would kill me, but I wanted you in my life any way I could get you. I felt like scum wanting someone else's wife, but I couldn't help it. There was no avoiding what I felt for you." Though she couldn't see him, he had to be on his knees now. His lips feathered over the skin right above her covered butt.

His raw confession shattered through her like glass, completely flaying her open. She'd had no idea he'd felt this way. Maybe she should have after the intense way he'd made love to her that night. "Kell—"

"Don't say anything. I just wanted you to know." His hands moved around to her front again, and in seconds he had her jeans off so that she was standing there in just her bra and panties.

She risked a glance over her shoulder to find him pushing up from his kneeling position. His pale eyes seemed darker, more intense, and his five o'clock shadow gave him a sexy, edgy quality that had her quivering with the need to jump him right there. Not to mention what he'd just admitted to her. She wanted to tell him how she felt, that she'd fallen hard for him. The house was fairly quiet, the only other noise the soft music he had playing trailing in from the living room.

She turned to face him. "Kell, I—"

"No. Talking." That was when she saw the vulnerability in his eyes. As if he was afraid of what she might say.

Before she could string more than a few words together, his fingers flexed around her hips and he lifted her onto the counter. With practically no clothing on, she felt so damn exposed and a little nervous about his reaction to her body. Before she'd been stretched out on the bed and the lighting had been sexy but they were under the bright lights of the kitchen. Nothing sexy about that. There was no hiding every little flaw she had.

When Kell let out a shudder, his gaze raking over her entire body from head to toe with an almost reverent look, something inside her cracked open. Beneath that worshipful gaze, she felt beautiful, cherished. Kell was everything she'd ever wanted in a man. Hell, more than she'd imagined.

Disobeying his order, she reached out to wrap her hand around the back of his neck and met his mouth in a hungry, frenzied kiss. She couldn't stop herself. The need to have him inside her, filling her, was too much. She was already so wet it was almost embarrassing and she wanted him to claim her in the way only he'd ever done. She wanted to be completely dominated by him, to watch his cock pumping in and out of her and to see his face as he climaxed inside her.

As their tongues stroked and teased each other, a loud pounding made her freeze. At first she couldn't figure out what the sound was until reality slowly registered. Someone was pounding on his front door. Kell cursed under his breath, his features murderous. "Someone better be dead," he muttered as he tore away from her.

Charlotte slid off the counter and started dressing as he continued cursing and practically stomped from the room. She figured it was one of the security guys she knew was still watching the house and she agreed with Kell. Someone better be freaking dead. She was so primed for Kell right now she knew it wouldn't take much for her to climax. Her nipples tightened pleasurably at the thought.

That feeling disappeared as she heard a loud female voice shouting. After making sure her clothes were on straight, Charlotte hurried out of the room toward the front of the house.

The front door was open and Kell was on the porch, his hands on the shoulders of the same blonde woman she'd seen leaving his house a few weeks ago. She wore a skimpy green dress despite the cooler weather, her mascara was smeared and by her glassy eyes she looked drunk or high on something. And she was shouting in Kell's face, her words nonsensical, as he tried to hold her away from him.

One of the security guys who'd guarded Charlotte last week was behind the woman, a black streak of paint or dirt across his entire face. What the hell had happened?

Charlotte had no clue what was going on, but turned to find her phone to call the police when the blonde spotted her. Her eyes filled with rage. "I've been fucking your boyfriend the past couple weeks whore, where have you been?"

Charlotte froze at the vile words, feeling as if she'd been slapped. When her dead husband's mistress had confronted her she'd been blindsided. Not because she was surprised by his infidelity but because of the animosity of the strange woman. It was the same now as the blonde continued screaming obscenities. For a brief moment, old insecurities bubbled up inside her, but she knew there was no way in hell that Kell had been with anyone the past couple weeks. Not after the way he'd just laid himself bare. Maybe she was stupid, but she trusted this man more than she ever had another man.

Kell cursed again as he and the other man hauled the woman away from the front door. Charlotte quickly shut it, not wanting that maniac anywhere near her son, then she quickly found her cell. As she was wrapping up her call with the police dispatcher, Kell opened the front door, the collar of his shirt distended and scratches on his neck. Her eyes widened in worry, but he gave a sharp shake of his head.

"I'll be back in a sec." He disappeared down the hall, then was back outside again.

Following him only as far as the entryway, Charlotte watched as he slid plastic tie things on her wrists. Whatever they were they must be sturdy because the woman couldn't seem to break them. Though she was certainly trying.

Kell turned, his gaze locking on hers. "Stay inside."

Frowning at his order, she did what he said anyway, not wanting him to be distracted. Seconds later he was inside, looking disheveled and frustrated.

"Are you okay?" She stepped toward him, worry flooding her.

His jaw tight, he nodded as he scrubbed a hand over his face. "I didn't sleep with that woman."

She blinked, surprised by the fear in his gaze. Fear that she wouldn't believe him. Her heart squeezed. "I know."

He stared at her for a long moment, his shoulders relaxing. "You do?"

She nodded. "You're not like Andrew. I know that."

It was almost like a weight lifted from him at her words. Before he could say anything else, she continued. "I called the police and they're on their way." As if on cue, the sound of sirens in the distance rent through the air.

"I called them too. Freaking nut job," he muttered.

"Who is she and what does she want?"

For a moment he looked embarrassed, then just resigned. "We went on a few dates—but I never slept with her," he interjected hastily, as if she'd be pissed about something he'd done in his past. "I ended things and apparently she's a total nut. She uh, spray painted your car and when one of the guys tried to stop her she spray painted him. I could be wrong but I'm betting she's behind your slashed tires too."

That actually made more sense, especially since the cartel had no issue with her and she'd never been able to figure out how anyone had found out where she'd been staying so quickly. Despite the insanity of the situation, she let out a shaky laugh. "Is it crazy that I'm actually relieved it's some nut job ex who trashed my car and not the Mexican cartel? I never thought I'd be saying *that*."

Kell pulled her into his arms, his grip around her tightening as she laid her head against his chest. She inhaled, loving the spicy, masculine scent she could easily get addicted to. "We'll press charges and so will the guard. She assaulted both of us and defaced your property. I doubt she'll do much time, but I'll also get a restraining order against her and see if Harrison can talk to the DA."

Charlotte breathed in his spicy scent, letting it ground her. "We'll figure everything out. At least I know life with you will never be boring," she murmured against his chest.

He went impossibly still for a moment but as the police siren grew louder he stepped back, his expression carefully guarded. She wasn't sure what she'd said to elicit that reaction, but she didn't have time to dwell on it. "I'm going to check on Reece but I'll be out here in a few minutes."

After kissing him, she hurried to the back of the house. By now she was a pro at filling out police reports. She just hoped this was the last one she would have to fill out for a long time.

CHAPTER ELEVEN

Cecil stuck to the shadows next to the empty house across the street from his intended target. He'd gotten damn lucky with the help of an old friend from high school. After managing to get a copy of the police report on Mateo's murder—no small feat in itself—he'd gotten the witness's name and phone number. For the past couple weeks his friend had been trying to track the damn thing. Of course Cecil had to lie to him about what it was for because if he'd told the truth—that he planned to eliminate the owner of the number—he'd have been out of luck.

Watching the spectacle of the crazy blonde woman across the street, he realized he might be able to pin the planned murder on someone else. Or at least he wouldn't be the only suspect once it all went down. What a fucking psycho.

The past couple weeks he'd been living in pay-by-the-hour motels and keeping a low profile and he'd been about to give up on her and just split town when his buddy had called with a hit.

A small part of him felt bad because she had a kid, but what the fuck ever. He'd grown up without a mom. Life wasn't fair.

The only thing holding him up now was the obvious guards she had. Something that surprised him. Unfortunately he hadn't been able to find out much about her. He could have had his friend get her info but that would have caused too many problems if the cops ever came sniffing around. Not to mention his buddy would have gotten nosy and probably figured out exactly why he was after her. As it was, Cecil had told him the woman owed him a shitload of money and he just wanted to collect his due.

He could hear sirens in the distance but he wasn't too worried. The house he was hiding near was empty. A for sale sign stood in the front yard and one of the windows in the back didn't have curtains or blinds, showing a clearly empty house. If he could figure out if the place was alarmed he might break in later. Once the cops had left of course.

The big guy who had been outside earlier strode back out with something in his hand. Cecil didn't know his name but it was clear that the guy lived in the house and that he had some sort of training. Either one of the men could have hurt the blonde but they were carefully restraining her. Cecil squinted, trying to see what was in the guy's hands. Flex-cuffs, he realized when the other man put them on the thrashing woman's wrists behind her back.

She had to be on something, acting all crazy like that. The front door opened again, and the dark-haired beauty, Charlotte Bastien according to the police report, stepped out, but only a few inches. She still hovered in the doorway but the big guy must have heard her because he turned and shook his head, saying something too low for Cecil to catch.

Immediately the woman did as he said and moments later, the guy followed. Having seen enough for the time being, Cecil slipped back into the shadows. He couldn't be sure but it looked like the woman lived there. Maybe with the guy. This was a really nice neighborhood and the fact that there had been a guard sitting across the street when the blonde maniac had showed up said that either she or the man she was with had serious money or connections. And she was being careful.

She couldn't be stupid. She had to know he was out there and a real threat. Normally people were easier to target, but all he'd have to do was watch and wait. No one could be protected all the time. Once she was alone or he created a situation where he could make her that way, he'd strike.

But he wouldn't make her suffer, and he'd try not to do it in front of her kid. He wasn't into torture or any of that shit. He just wanted her dead so he could get the hell out of town and far away from Renaldo Diaz. One of the boys from the gang had told him Diaz was definitely hunting him and it was only a matter of time before that bastard found him.

Right now he was living on borrowed time unless he could flee Miami and start over. A new name, new city, new fucking life.

CHAPTER TWELVE

Charlotte tried not to drool at the sight of Kell's muscular arms as he leaned against the window of the driver's side of her vehicle. Well *his* actually, since he was letting her drive his truck. The word 'whore' had been spray painted across her car so she wasn't driving it anywhere until it was cleaned. She'd just gotten new tires and replaced her broken window from the previous damage and she really hoped she wouldn't have to take her vehicle to the repair shop again after this.

The way he was propped up with his arms crossed over the top of the frame with him looking in at her was way too sexy. After that nut job had been arrested last night they hadn't taken up where they'd left off in the kitchen. Reece had been fussy all night and she'd been too damn tired to even think about sex. Luckily Kell had been a huge help with their son. Amazing what a difference having another person around to help out could make.

"I don't like letting you go alone," he murmured, almost sulking. Which made him impossibly adorable. She didn't want to go either, but she'd put her life on hold for weeks and it was time to get into a normal routine. And she wasn't missing this meeting.

"I'm not alone. I've got a guard at all times." Something she wasn't complaining about. She was still freaked out that a murderer she'd seen was still out there, but she couldn't remain in hiding forever. Vincent was in an SUV in the driveway right behind her and he'd be her shadow all day. While he might look like a pretty boy she also knew he'd been a SEAL and it was clear Kell trusted him. That alone spoke volumes. "Besides, you can't miss this. It's too important."

He gritted his teeth for a moment, but finally nodded. "I know."

There was a one-day local job for a senator's son and the man had handpicked Kell because he knew him from his days with the FBI. Kell had saved the man's life five years ago and considering how new he was with Red Stone there was no way he could turn this job down. It would look great for him at work and she didn't want to take that away from him. Not when she was perfectly fine and protected. "I've got my phone on me and I swear I'll answer it no matter what—except during my interview, but I'll text you right before I go in and as I'm leaving." She might not plan on going back to teaching for a few years but the past couple weeks had made it clear she needed to be doing something outside of the house for her own sanity.

She wanted to start working as a tutor at a local community center. It would only be a couple nights a week and her mother had agreed to help out with babysitting when Kell couldn't watch Reece. Even though it was a volunteer position she still had to do a face-to-face interview.

Reece started fussing in the backseat so she leaned over to Kell and gave him a quick kiss. "I need to get him to my mom's and you need to get ready."

He looked hesitant but finally nodded. "You'll answer any time I call?"

Fighting a grin, she nodded. "Yes."

"Okay." He motioned to Vincent who then reversed, leaving her enough room to back up. At first she'd been surprised that he wasn't riding with them, but Kell had told her it was harder to tail two vehicles and they wanted to see if anyone followed her. Plus he'd given her a small gun for the drive over—though she wouldn't be bringing it into the community center with her.

She waved at Kell as she drove away. She was having lunch with her mom, then leaving Reece for a few hours so she could do the interview. By the time she picked him up and returned home Kell would probably be there too.

She was looking forward to that way too much. Butterflies took flight in her stomach any time she thought of him or what she hoped would happen between them tonight.

The drive to her mom's house didn't take long and even though she invited Vincent to have lunch with them he declined, keeping watch over the backyard as she and her mother ate on the lanai. It was a clear sunny day without a cloud in the sky but it was in the low 50s with no humidity. A rarity in Florida, even in February.

"So...how are things with you and Reece's father?" her mom asked carefully as she sat back against the padded sling rocker chair.

Unlike the majority of her friends and even her father and sister, her mother had known about Charlotte's problems with Andrew. While they might not be as close as Charlotte would like, her mother was surprisingly intuitive sometimes.

"Ah, good." Okay, that didn't come close to covering what was going on with them.

Her mother was silent for a moment as she regarded Charlotte with dark brown eyes so similar to her own. "Are you sleeping with him?"

More surprised than anything, Charlotte's mouth almost dropped open. She leaned back against her own chair, her half-eaten Panini forgotten. "Not yet."

"A man doesn't ask a woman and her son to move in with him without wanting anything more serious. He might have said this arrangement was temporary, but he has every intention of making it permanent—and I think you want that too."

"I'm scared." Even saying the words aloud felt freeing. She wasn't just scared, she was terrified. What happened if she let Kell into her life then things exploded in their faces? They had a son to think about and if she was being really honest, Charlotte knew she was risking her heart. And Kell had the ability to shred it to ribbons.

"That's understandable, but clearly this man isn't like your husband, who liked the young woman you were more than the woman you grew into."

Charlotte blinked as more shock punched through her. "What?"

Her mother smiled faintly as she picked up her iced tea. "The last Christmas you were here with Andrew, I could see the tension between you two, the way you were growing apart. It was subtle, but...you weren't the same woman he'd married and my guess is Andrew resented it. Maybe even tried to make you feel guilty about growing into your own person."

"You're not far off the mark," Charlotte murmured, her mother's words hitting their target with piercing accuracy.

"Well, you're not the same girl who married him. You're older, a lot smarter and you need to trust your instincts with Kellen."

At that Charlotte smiled. She sometimes called him by his full name, but it was rare. "You can call him Kell when you meet him."

Her mother shifted slightly on her seat, turning her chin up in that familiar fashion that always made Charlotte smile. "I'll call him by the name his mother gave him. Speaking of which, when can I expect to meet him? We'd like to have all of you over for dinner soon." Yeah, she wasn't so much asking Charlotte as ordering.

She couldn't blame her. The past two weeks would have been impossible for them to meet since Charlotte had been hiding out at Lizzy and Porter's place. And she hadn't been ready for them to meet Kell before then. Not before she got a hold on her feelings for him.

"I need to check what his schedule is, but maybe this weekend if he's free." With that, Charlotte knew she was going to take the chance that might get her heart broken. She had to make a go of things with Kell or she'd regret it for the rest of her life.

She might not have been able to admit it to him, but she loved him. She'd realized it the night before when he'd had that panicked, vulnerable expression over the lunatic blonde woman. He'd been so worried Charlotte would think he'd betrayed her that she'd known in a bone deep way that Kell would never intentionally hurt her. He'd rather talk or argue than turn to someone else.

And her mom was right, Kell wanted the woman she was. Not a young, inexperienced girl barely a woman.

Sighing, she glanced at the slim watch on her wrist and realized she needed to head out soon. Her father was watching Reece so she and her mother could enjoy lunch, but she wanted to kiss her son before she left too. The community center was only twenty minutes away but she wanted to account for traffic in case there was any.

* * *

Cecil crept down the hallway of a place he was very familiar with. It had been difficult but he'd managed to follow the SUV tailing the witness. Once he'd realized she had a shadow of her own, all he'd had to do was follow that guy.

The woman had gone to a very wealthy neighborhood this afternoon so he hadn't followed her past the gated community. Instead he'd just waited, knowing she'd have to leave sometime. He'd tailed people in the past before killing them and the watching and waiting was always a pain, but he'd stolen a luxury sedan and switched the plates so at least he was driving in comfort.

Now she was at the community center he'd frequented as a teenager. It was where he'd first started selling drugs. Since it was a Wednesday and not quite three o'clock yet, the place was empty for the most part. Which was perfect for him. The fewer witnesses the better.

Cecil had watched as the tall, intimidating looking guard for the woman had followed her inside. The man had scanned the parking lot, watching for any threats, but Cecil hadn't parked in the main lot. He'd been across the street in hiding. Once they'd gone inside, he'd slashed the SUVs tires. When he ran, he wasn't going to risk the chance of anyone pursuing. Because after today, he was gone from Miami for good.

His sneakers were silent against the terrazzo flooring as he rounded the corner into another hallway. He couldn't be sure, but the only reason for a clearly wealthy woman like Charlotte to be here was because she wanted to donate money or volunteer. Either way, she'd be in the main office.

Lucky for him, there was another room that connected to it through one of the rooms for the five-year-olds and younger. The woman who ran this place liked to be close to the little ones in case there was ever trouble. She'd been running this place for over twenty years so he knew how things worked with her.

Slipping into the empty room with desks and colorful drawings on the walls, he immediately pulled out his stocking mask and tugged it over his face. He'd dyed his hair dark brown for other potential witnesses, but he needed his face covered this time. From the attached office he could hear murmured female voices. He knew he was taking a risk, but it had to be done now. If the woman was separated from her guard—and he was pretty sure the guy was sitting in the anterior office since he'd come in with her—it was his best opportunity.

The door had a glass pane in it, letting light through but it was a thick glass, making it impossible to see inside. Testing the door, he internally smiled when it twisted. He drew his gun and raised it as he stepped inside.

Charlotte sat on one side of a desk and Lana Gonzalez, the woman who ran the place, sat on the other. They stared at him with wide eyes, both clearly speechless. When it appeared the witness might scream, he let out a low growling sound. "Stand up and quietly come with me or I'll wait until the kids get here and start shooting randomly," he whispered. He wouldn't actually do that, but he needed them terrified enough to do what he said. Since he wasn't sure if the woman's guard was in the other connected room he wasn't taking a chance of being overheard by shouting.

Knowing the threat against children would keep them quiet, he kept his gun hand steady as he slowly backed up. The women followed him. Once they were in the hallway he pressed his gun into Charlotte's spine and shoved her forward. The Gonzalez woman was in front of her, terror in her dark eyes.

Even though she couldn't see him clearly because of the mask, he kept his gaze trained on the community center director. "We're going to walk out of here quietly and neither of you are going to make a sound or I'll pump this bitch full of bullets. Understand?"

She nodded and Cecil risked a quick glance over his shoulder to make sure they weren't being followed. It was clear.

"You don't have to do this," Charlotte said quietly, her voice teary.

He pushed the gun into her. "Quiet. Move." Another hard shove and the women were hurrying down the hall in front of him. Once they'd rounded the corner, he told them to stop and opened the ladies' bathroom door. "In," he commanded.

The women walked in and he tossed a pair of flex-cuffs to Lana. "Hook yourself to the handicap rail," he demanded.

It was clear she didn't want to, but he put the barrel of the gun to Charlotte's head, spurring her into action.

Once she was secure, he grabbed Charlotte's arm and dragged her from the room and down another hallway.

"I have a young son," she pleaded, her voice shaky, as they stepped out into the sunlight of the parking lot. He took off his mask, not caring if she saw him now. Plus now he needed to blend in.

"Shut the fuck up or I'll make you suffer." He wouldn't but he needed her quiet until he could get her somewhere private. He planned to hide her body so the police wouldn't know she was dead for at least a few days. They'd waste time searching for her, which would throw some of the heat off him while he made his escape.

He hurried her across the paved parking lot onto the side street where he'd parked his stolen car. There were a few new vehicles parked along the curb, but the street was quiet. Perfect. Popping the trunk, he started to shove her inside when a scuffling sound alerted him that he wasn't alone.

She started screaming, punching at him from behind, her hard fists slamming into his spine and shoulders. But she wasn't his problem. As he turned, a fist connected with his jaw. For a moment he saw a bright flash of light as pain exploded in his face. He was aware of dropping his gun as another fist slammed into his nose. More excruciating pain.

Then, blackness.

CHAPTER THIRTEEN

As the elevator he was in headed to the parking garage of the Red Stone Security building, Kell dialed Charlotte's cell phone again for the third time, but got nothing. It rang five times then went to voicemail. She'd texted him letting him know she was going into the interview and would put her phone on silent, but that had been almost an hour ago. How long did an interview for a volunteer position take anyway? He didn't want to bug her or try to smother her, but after the past couple weeks he couldn't curb his overprotective nature.

The security job for the day had been postponed until Friday. Their principal had been delayed because of personal issues Kell didn't give a crap about. He just cared that he'd been called into work a job and now didn't need to. He could have been Charlotte's guard today rather than Vincent. And possibly gotten some much needed alone time with her before she picked Reece up from her parents.

"Screw it," he muttered to himself as he started to dial Vincent. He hadn't wanted to harass his friend since he was more than capable of protecting Charlotte.

But right now Kell wasn't feeling rational. Before he could dial, his phone buzzed in his hand.

"Charlotte's been taken," Vincent said.

Horror slammed through him, making him stumble as he exited into the quiet garage. "Tell me everything." His voice was hoarse, clipped.

"A masked man took Charlotte and her interviewer at gunpoint. There's another entrance to the office I didn't know about. I'm sorry man—"

"I don't care. What happened?" He raced to one of the company SUVs he still had the keys for from the days cancelled job. Vincent could make all the damn apologies in the world after they got Charlotte back.

"The guy cuffed the other woman in a bathroom and took Charlotte. I heard the woman screaming and found her unharmed. By the time I got out to the parking lot the fucker had slashed my tires. The woman says it was only one man who took her, but I saw two vehicles—one sedan and one SUV tearing away from the road. I got their license plates and have Charlotte's truck keys, but they're gone."

"I'm going to patch Lizzy into this conversation, but did you grab her purse or anything?" If Vincent had his truck keys he could only assume he'd retrieved them from Charlotte's purse. Kell started the SUV but remained where he was, having no place to go and feeling completely useless. His heart beat an erratic tattoo against his chest, but he had to stay focused and calm until Charlotte was safe. Either the cartel, the 19th Street Gang, or Cecil Talley had taken her. None were good options.

"Yeah. It was in the office when I found it empty."

"What's in it?"

There was a brief shuffling on the other end while Kell used the add participant function to dial Lizzy's direct number. He'd just seen her as he left Harrison's office so he prayed she was still upstairs.

"Yeah?" she said.

"Lizzy, it's Kell and Vincent. Charlotte's been taken."

The other woman sucked in a sharp breath. "What do you need?"

"Vincent, did you find her phone?" he asked.

"Just the company one, but not the red one I saw her using to text you earlier."

Thank God. Kell didn't let one ounce of relief slide through him though. Not yet. "Lizzy, I need you to track her if possible." Courtesy of Red Stone's technology he'd put trackers on both her phones. He just hoped she had hers with her. If they could just get a general area Kell would rip the entire fucking city apart to find her. She had to be alive because he refused to believe otherwise. Absolutely refused.

The fear was clawing its way through him, trying to shred him apart, but they'd taken her. They hadn't killed her outright, which would have been the easiest thing to do.

"Okay...just one sec...her cell's moving down Brickell right now at forty-five miles per hour. Whoever she's with, they're sticking to the speed limit."

Kell sped out of his parking space, his tires squealing as he zoomed to the nearest exit. Lizzy continued giving them directions, both he and Vincent on their way to find her. There was no way he was getting off the phone to call the police. Charlotte was his and he was more than trained to find her. Both he and Vincent were.

"Lizzy, let Harrison know what's going on so he can get a team together, but no cops. We're taking care of this our way." For all he knew there were more dirty cops on the force, but he didn't want them involved for more reasons than just that. Whoever had taken Charlotte was going to die.

His friend tried to apologize again, but Kell cut him off. Right now wasn't the time for any of that shit. Now he had to keep his head on straight and focus on his only goal. Finding Charlotte and bringing her home safely.

* * *

Charlotte felt as if someone had taken a two-by-four to her head. Groggily, she struggled to open her eyes. A bright light was shining directly in them so she moved her head and it immediately subsided, letting her start to make out shapes.

That was when she realized she was in the trunk of an unmoving car and the light wasn't exactly bright, but her face had been right in front of the tiny bulb. Not that any of that was important.

Rolling over onto her side, she brought her hand up to her face to brush her hair out of the way only to find her hands bound in front of her. As she struggled to remember what happened, she heard a gurgled moaning coming from somewhere close. The trunk of the car was cracked open a fraction, letting the noise in.

It sounded like a wounded animal crying out for help and made all the hairs on her arms stand up. The eerie cry was...pitiful and made something primal inside her want to hide. She froze as she heard a man's voice speaking in Spanish. The words were low, guttural and the voice was raspy. It was followed by more moaning.

Then a sharp cry of obvious pain. She wanted to curl into a ball and cover her ears so she'd never have to hear something so creepy again, but getting the hell out of there was all that mattered.

She clearly remembered Cecil Talley kidnapping her at gunpoint then trying to shove her into a trunk. Someone else had been there too, but she hadn't gotten a good look at them before something had struck her in the head. After that she didn't remember anything else but someone had definitely tied her up.

Pushing up, she struggled to sit, her head hitting the inside of the trunk. She bit back the instinctive cry of pain, but as she struck the lid, it creaked as it popped open.

She froze at the sight in front of her. She had to be in a warehouse of some sort, but that wasn't what was shocking.

A bruised and bleeding Talley was tied to a chair, his face swollen, almost unrecognizable and...oh, Lord, were those fingers on the ground lying in a pool of blood? Her stomach roiled but she kept it together as the masked man with the machete-type weapon turned to look at her.

He wore a red and black mask that looked like something from Halloween. She could only see his eyes, dark and savage, looking back at her. His long-sleeved T-shirt, cargo pants and boots were all black.

Run!

Jerking out of her shock, she gave in to the urge to flee. She managed to swing one leg, then the other over the trunk. With her wrists tied together in front of her it was a struggle and she fell to her knees. Pain ricocheted through her at the abrupt fall, but she shoved up and started running.

Charlotte made it four steps before a huge body slammed into her, twisting them until he had her pinned up against the car.

Breathing hard against her ear, she could feel the man's elevated heartbeat against her back. Pure terror spiked through her and she tried to struggle but he held a knife to her throat. She went completely immobile. The blade didn't dig into her skin, but it wouldn't take much for him to kill her. He could do it so quickly, with one slice. Facing her own mortality, all she could picture were Kell and Reece's faces. She wanted to tell Kell she loved him and hold her baby one more time. The thought of her son growing up without her made her want to sob, but she held herself in check, not wanting to give the man any excuse to slice her open.

"I didn't expect you to wake up before I was done," he rasped against her ear, his breath hot. There was a hint of an accent to his guttural words.

"I haven't seen your face," she managed to gasp out through her pounding fear.

"I know. It's the only reason I'm letting you live." It took a long moment for his words to register. A burst of relief flooded her, but before she could respond he continued. "You tell anyone you saw me here, your son will grow up without a mother. And I know *exactly* who you are Charlotte Bastien. You woke up tied in the trunk, found a dead man outside it and ran for help. Easy enough to remember?"

She hadn't seen his face anyway and even if she had, she knew deep down she wouldn't tell a soul what he looked like. She wasn't letting Reece grow up without her or putting him in danger. Nothing was worth that. "Yes," she said immediately.

Suddenly the weight was gone and she heard soft footsteps walking away. Though it terrified her to do it, she looked over her shoulder.

The masked man was standing behind the abused Talley, his knife right at the dying man's throat and his dark eyes directly on hers. He slit the man's throat as he stared at her. Charlotte didn't pause as she turned and sprinted across the concrete floor into more darkness, her heart racing out of control.

She had no clue where she was going or even where she was, and she didn't care as long as it was out of *here*. She could see a faint light from an open oversized door big enough to let cars in. City lights or moonlight, she couldn't tell and she didn't care.

It represented freedom.

Too terrified to look over her shoulders to see if the man had changed his mind about letting her live, she pushed on until she burst out into the quiet night air.

To the right she could see water. Biscayne Bay maybe, she couldn't tell. To her left and in front of her, a parking lot and more warehouses stretched out. Everything was so quiet, the only thing she could hear was the slamming of her own heart as she veered left across the parking lot.

It had to lead to a road. Or she hoped it did. As she ran, the sound of tires squealing had her looking over her shoulder. Two SUVs came into view as they tore across the lot.

A new surge of panic punched through her, flaying all her nerve endings. Maybe the man had changed his mind and had sent more people after her.

There was a sound of screeching tires, then she heard her name being shouted.

"Charlotte!" Oh God, it was Kell.

She stumbled, her sandals catching on gravel as she tried to stop her momentum. She started running for him, the dim moonlight her only guide in the darkness. Before she'd made it five feet he was there, pulling her into his arms and kissing her face. She wanted to wrap her arms around him, but couldn't because of her bonds.

All she could do was sob into his neck, more thankful than she'd ever been to be alive. A small part of her wondered if she should be embarrassed but there was no way in hell she could hold all these raw emotions in now. So she let all her fear and pain out on Kell's shirt and let him embrace her and rub his hand down her back as he murmured soothing words she couldn't understand but made her feel better just the same.

CHAPTER FOURTEEN

Charlotte was still shaky, but after hours at that warehouse then at the police station, she'd lost most of the original terror coursing through her system. Now she just wanted to sleep for a week, but soaking in Kell's bathtub was helping. Thankfully her mother had offered to keep Reece overnight and since her sister had checked herself into a rehab clinic and wasn't there, Charlotte was incredibly grateful and more than willing to let her mother watch him. Right now she didn't have the emotional energy for much, and picking him up in the middle of the night would have just upset his sleep.

The bathroom door opening made a squeaking sound, but it triggered her panic as she expected to see a masked intruder with a knife coming to finish her off. She started to push up, but sank back against the sunken-in tub, letting her head fall back in relief when she saw Kell. Wearing dark jeans that molded to muscular thighs and a plain T-shirt that showed off everything she wanted to kiss and run her hands over, the man looked good enough to eat.

He had a glass of red wine in his hand and a half-smile on that harsh face. Kneeling on the tile next to her, he set the glass on the edge, his eyes straying to the water. He didn't even try to disguise his lust, which made her smile despite the residual tension in her body. She'd added bubbles but they'd long since dissipated, barely covering any of her. Not that she cared at this point. Kell had seen all of her and tonight—technically this morning since it was after two—they were taking the next step in their relationship. He might not realize it, but they were. After almost dying she wasn't turning her back on what they could have. Risking heartbreak was worth it to be with him for however long it lasted.

"Just heard from Carlson. They've scoured the area and haven't been able to find anyone. Whoever tortured Talley didn't leave any evidence behind. You're just lucky you were unconscious for everything." He scrubbed a tired hand over his face.

Charlotte swallowed hard, but she kept her gaze on Kell. She hadn't had a chance to tell him the truth yet and there was no way she was telling anyone else but him. "I...spoke to the man who killed Talley. He was there right before I ran."

Kell's jaw was tight, his expression fierce and primal. "You escaped him?"

She shook her head and pushed back the memory of what she'd seen the masked man do. "No. He let me go. He hadn't thought I'd wake up I guess but when I got out of the trunk I didn't make it far before he stopped me.

He said..." She swallowed again, trying to force the words past her tight throat. "That it would be a shame for my son to grow up without a mother. Then he told me that I wasn't to tell anyone I'd seen him there. He was wearing a mask anyway so there's no way I could identify him, but...even if I could, I wouldn't." She felt almost ashamed admitting it, but she wasn't going to put her son's life in danger over the death of a drug-dealing bastard who'd planned to kill her anyway.

Kell surprised her then, his hand shaking as he took the wine glass and downed the contents in one gulp. "Fuck!" He shook his head, as if trying to clear it before that laser-like focus was on her again, his pale green eyes piercing her. "We're not telling anyone about this. I could be wrong, but Renaldo Diaz is rumored to be in town and he likes to torture his victims before he kills them. It's part of his MO. He also grew up without a mother and raised his only brother—the one Talley killed. He had to have been hunting Talley for revenge and he doesn't like to hurt women. It's apparently part of his own fucked up moral code, and thank God for it."

That didn't make Charlotte feel much better, but she was glad she'd gotten the truth off her chest. She'd been carrying it around since the warehouse, desperate to tell Kell but afraid someone would overhear. Now that she'd gotten that out of the way, there was one more thing she needed to say. "I love you, Kell."

At those words, he completely froze, his big body going almost preternaturally still. He shook his head. "Don't," he rasped out, looking haunted.

She frowned at his response. "Don't what? Tell you the truth? I love you, and after tonight I'm not holding anything back from you ever again."

"You've had a bad night—hell, the past couple weeks have been hard—so don't say anything in the heat of the moment. You don't mean it." His expression went blank, as if he was trying to guard himself from her.

Part of her felt responsible for that because she'd been trying to shut him out until now but it also infuriated her. Standing in the tub, she let the water run down her and savored the feeling of Kell's hungry gaze roving over her entire body. The cool air and his heated look made her nipples tighten into little beads. "Don't tell me what I do or do not feel." Stepping over the tub, she snatched the blue towel he'd laid out and wrapped it around herself.

He stood, his expression wary. "I told you I loved you a year ago and you kicked me out of your life."

Charlotte heard the hurt in his voice and wanted to erase it. Closing the distance between them, she tentatively slid her arms around him, lacing her fingers together behind his back and pulling him close.

His body was rigid, but at least he didn't resist. That would have killed her. And he was definitely aroused.

His big arms slid around her and even through the towel, his erection pressed firmly against her lower abdomen, making it clear that he wanted her—at least physically.

"I know and I'm sorry. That was a very dark time in my life. My husband had died, I'd just had his infidelity thrown in my face and then there was you. I never expected that night and to realize what an explosive attraction we had...well, you were there. You know how intense that night was. I was still trying to come to grips with what we'd done and..." She trailed off, not wanting to say the words.

"Then I confessed that I loved you and had for almost as long as I knew you." He sounded torn up as he spoke.

She reached up, gently cupping his stubble covered cheek, wanting him to understand. "I had no idea."

"I know." His pale eyes darkened, filling with hunger as his gaze strayed to her lips.

"Well, I love you now and that's not going to change. And I'm not moving out in a couple months either. You're stuck with me." She knew the statement was bold, but she also knew Kell wanted her and Reece there. After the way she'd freaked out on him a year ago she wanted to reassure him that they weren't going anywhere.

"I wasn't planning on letting you leave," he murmured.

"Really?"

He shook his head, his expression turning scorching. "Nope. I'd planned on using a lot of sex to convince you to stay."

His words went straight to the growing ache between her legs. Yeah, she could definitely get on board with that. Dropping her hands, she reached between their bodies and loosened her towel, letting it fall to the floor. "Why don't you start convincing me now?"

A shudder rippled through him as he grabbed her behind, lifting her up against his body. Immediately she wrapped her legs around him, wishing he was naked too.

She was already wet and aching for him. The rough denim of his jeans rubbing against her clit had her inner walls clenching with the need to be filled by him.

As their mouths met, she felt almost frenzied wanting to touch him everywhere. His kisses weren't gentle or sweet this time, they were frantic and needy. She was vaguely aware he was moving them as they stepped into the dimness of his bedroom. Tugging at his shirt, she had it over his head right before her back hit the cool sheets.

She didn't have a chance to visually appreciate his body before his mouth sought hers again. Wrapping her hands around his back, she grinded her hips against his as her fingers dug into his skin.

His body tensed above hers, all his muscles pulling taut as she continued rolling her hips against his. Her not-so-subtle actions made it clear she wanted him inside her and was tired of waiting.

When her hands moved lower and she tried to slide them under his jeans to latch onto his tight backside, he reached behind his body, grabbed her wrists and had them pinned above her head in seconds. Breathing hard, she opened her eyes to stare up at him. "What are you doing?"

"Slowing you down," he murmured, his fingers flexing around her wrists where he held her securely in place.

Not that she struggled against him. She enjoyed the feel of him dominating her. Had loved it a year ago. He'd been so raw and uninhibited that it had been easy for her to let go too.

He nipped her bottom lip, pulling it between his teeth before he kissed his way up her jaw to her earlobe. His breath was warm against her skin, sending shivers of desire spiraling through her. When he pulled the sensitive lobe between his teeth, she moaned, arching her breasts into his chest.

Her nipples brushed against his strength and his smattering of dark hair. The feel of it rubbing against her breasts was just soft enough to send her senses into overdrive. After the past few months she was overly sensitive, but this was perfect and torturous at the same time. "I need you in me," she managed to gasp out as his free hand cupped her breast.

He held her firmly, rubbing his thumb around her nipple, but never actually touching it because he knew how sensitive she was. His complete thoughtfulness made her even wetter. She wondered what she'd done to deserve a man like Kell.

The feel of his calloused hand on her was about to send her into overload when his movements slowed, becoming even more teasing.

"Hold on to the headboard," he murmured against her neck where he'd been kissing and raking his teeth across her skin.

"Okay." She would do any damn thing he wanted right now if he brought her to orgasm.

As soon as she clutched onto it, his hand strayed right between her legs, cupping her mound in a completely possessive grip.

So damn slowly, he slid a finger inside her. Unable to stop herself, she rolled her hips, trying to force him to move faster, to give her more. Lord, she wanted more. Everything he could give her.

"I love how reactive you are," he murmured against her breast as he licked the underside of it.

She was, but only for him. The man had the ability to turn her on like no one else. Unwilling to drag this out any longer, she removed her hands from the headboard and clutched his shoulders.

He looked up, his green eyes flashing. "I thought I said to hold onto the headboard."

That dominating note in his voice sent a shiver streaking through her. But... "Not now. You can tease me all night, but now I just need you in me." After the insanity of the night she felt almost desperate for that connection.

He must have read something on her face because he pushed off her and shoved his jeans off—commando underneath. Her gaze settled on his cock and her entire body tingled with the thought of him pushing deep inside her. Over and over until she was coming around him.

When he started to open the nightstand drawer she realized what he was doing and partially pushed up. "I'm on the pill." And she hadn't been with anyone since him. Something he knew.

His hand froze on the drawer, his eyes turning hot as he let his hand fall away. "I was serious when I said I hadn't been with anyone since you."

"I know." She was starting to find that Kell didn't lie about anything to her. He'd admitted he loved her after their first night of sex.

While he hadn't said the words again, she understood why and she knew they'd come eventually. The fact that he hadn't slept with anyone since her told her everything she needed to know. Kell was a one woman kind of man. And she was his woman.

Always.

At her words, another shudder went through him and before she could react, he was covering her again, his big body stretched out over hers like a warm embrace. His fingers slid into the curtain of her hair as his mouth crushed hers in that sexy, frenzied way she knew she'd never get enough of.

He held the back of her head gently even though she could feel the leashed power thrumming through him. He was holding back. For her. She was still freaked out after everything that had happened and he was trying to be gentle.

Wrapping her legs around him, she dug her heels into his ass and grinded against him, trying to force him inside her.

A deep rumble escaped him as he pulled his head back. "Greedy and impatient. It's one of the hundred things I love about you."

His softly spoken words speared her as he buried his cock in her in one smooth thrust. Her back arched at the welcome intrusion, her inner walls immediately adjusting and molding around his thick length. She sucked in a deep breath, trying to ground herself, but it was damn near impossible.

The love she saw shining in his gaze combined with the feel of his cock was almost too much.

When he started slowly thrusting, she reached for him, needing to feel his strength covering her. Needing to be reminded that she was alive and so was he. They were both here and had a second chance at a life together. One she was grabbing with both hands.

She slid her hands over his shoulders as his mouth met hers. He teased open the seam of her lips, lightly biting and kissing her with erotic flicks of his tongue and teeth. His strokes started out smooth but the longer he thrust into her, the more unsteady he became.

A wild tension bunched inside her as her lower abdomen tightened. Her inner walls clenched convulsively around him with each stroke as she pushed closer and closer to the edge. But it wasn't enough. She needed a little extra stimulation.

As if he read exactly what she wanted, he reached between their bodies and tweaked her clit. He pressed down, rubbing in tight little circles that drove her crazy. Her orgasm punched into her, taking over all her senses as the pleasure ricocheted to all her nerve endings. It completely shattered her from the inside out.

While she was riding through her climax, his hit with more intensity. Tearing his mouth from hers, he buried his face against her neck, his shout primal as he emptied himself inside her in long, hard thrusts.

She wasn't sure how long they lay there like that, with her arms and legs wrapped around him and his face buried in her neck, but eventually he pushed up, his pale eyes a shade darker. "I love you, Charlotte."

His words washed over her, bathing her in the truth of them. Her heart seized to hear them from him again. "I love you too." It was one of the few things in her life she was absolutely sure of.

He dropped a soft kiss on her lips before leaning over to the nightstand. Considering they'd just made love without a condom she couldn't imagine what he was doing. But when he pulled out a small, red box the reality slammed into her. He...couldn't be, could he?

Still half-hard inside her, he laid the box on her chest and flipped it open to reveal a very shiny emerald cut diamond ring. She wasn't an expert but it looked to be at least a carat and a half and it was nearly colorless. Swallowing hard, she looked up into his eyes to find that vulnerable look there.

The one she never wanted to see on his face again. "Maybe I should have waited, but—"

"Yes." Okay, he hadn't actually asked, but his cock was inside her and he'd placed an engagement ring on her naked body. Close enough.

His lips quirked up as all worry fled his gaze. "I didn't ask anything yet."

She frowned but before she could formulate a response, he lifted her left hand and slid the ring on her ring finger. It was a perfect fit. Tears filled her eyes but as he kissed her, they immediately dried. Now wasn't the time for any more tears. Now was the time for new beginnings, the start of a life together as a family.

CHAPTER FIFTEEN

Charlotte held Reece close to her chest as she sat on one of the cushioned lounge chairs in her and Kell's backyard. The pool was pristine and glistening, though unused because of the cool weather. None of the many people at the barbeque cared though, everyone was eating, drinking and having a good time. There were at least twenty people who had showed up, most of whom she'd met by now.

It had only been a week since her kidnapping, but she'd already started making changes to the house, including buying actual patio furniture for the massive backyard. He was a little annoyed that she was using her own money, but that wasn't an argument he'd ever win. Besides, they'd be joining their accounts in the next year anyway once they got married.

She was pretty sure that deep down Kell didn't actually care what she did as long as she was in his bed every night. And sometimes during the day. She flushed as she remembered how he'd taken her on the living room floor that morning while their son had still been sleeping.

Noel, Travis's fiancé, sat on the edge of the lounge chair next to Charlotte and held out her hands with a pleading look. "Just for a few more minutes?"

Smiling, she handed the other woman a cooing Reece who just blinked those big green eyes adoringly at the other woman. Charlotte had barely gotten a chance to hold her own son all day because everyone at the barbeque had wanted to. Not that she was complaining. Everyone was so gentle with him and he was completely eating up all the attention.

"So when are you going to come by my coffee shop?" Noel asked as she gently rocked Reece—who was trying to pull her dangly hoop earrings.

"Now that we're finally getting into a normal routine, probably next week. And I promise to bring Reece," she said before the other woman could say anything.

Grinning, Noel leaned back in the chair and cuddled him closer. "I could just eat him up. I love the way babies smell and feel and..." A soft, private smile crossed her features for just a second, but Charlotte knew what she'd seen.

"Oh my...are you pregnant?" she whispered.

Noel looked startled for a moment, then nodded, her grin huge. "Yes, but don't tell anyone. I'm only six weeks along and we don't want to announce it until after the wedding. My brothers will freak otherwise. And you better be coming."

"I will." It was in two weeks, which seemed like very good timing if Noel wanted to fit into her wedding dress.

Charlotte had already asked her parents to babysit. With her sister out of the house and in rehab for a while, her parents had really stepped up with Reece and she was letting them spend as much time with their grandson as they wanted. Once her sister was finally discharged from the expensive rehab center, Charlotte would have to make a decision about letting her be around Reece when he was at her parents but that was a future worry.

"Who's that?" Charlotte asked quietly as her gaze strayed to an older man talking to Lana Gonzalez—who thankfully had given her the volunteer position despite the kidnapping craziness.

Noel turned around then snickered. "That's Keith Caldwell, the father of the Caldwell brothers and majority owner in Red Stone Security. He almost never comes to these things. I bet he's glad he decided to now. Gah, look at the man."

Charlotte silently agreed as she watched Lana work her magic on the older man. Lana was in her forties and she guessed Caldwell was close to sixty, but sparks were flying between them.

Kell appeared from the throng of people eating, drinking and enjoying themselves and pulled her to her feet. "We need to talk," he murmured.

Travis sat down next to Noel and immediately took Reece from her. Charlotte wanted to take him, but Kell tugged her along the stones lining the pool until they were on the far side and relatively alone. "Reece will be fine," he murmured when she looked over her shoulder.

She knew he would be, but she still got a little nervous if he was out of her sight for too long. She figured that would probably be standard for a while after her terrifying brush with death. When his hands settled protectively on her hips and he pulled her close, she looked back at him. "What's going on?"

For the first time in a week Kell finally looked as if he was relaxing. That definitely had to be a good sign.

"Carlson let Harrison know that the rumor on the street is Renaldo Diaz has left the country. Likely gone back to Mexico. If he was going to make a move on us, he'd have done it by now."

Charlotte let out a shaky breath, feeling a ton of pressure lift from her chest. Even though the man she'd seen killing Cecil had let her go, she'd still been looking over her shoulder everywhere she went. "That's great news."

"Well, I've got even more good news. After Monique was arrested, her fingerprints were matched to an unsolved fire a few years ago. Turns out she tried to burn down her ex-boyfriend's house while he was still in it. She'll do some time but it sounds like the DA might push to have her institutionalized. Either way, she's not our problem anymore either."

At the news that the woman who had trashed her car would be going away too, Charlotte wrapped her arms around Kell's neck and kissed him hard. Living with him the past week had been an easier transition than she'd imagined, but there had been those dark clouds hanging over their lives. As they lifted, she realized she'd never been happier in her life. With the son and man she loved more than anything, she finally felt at peace with the world. She was going to start her volunteer schedule next week and planned to stay with it until Reece was old enough for school. Then she would return to teaching—unless of course they had another baby in the meantime. Something Kell had mentioned last night, but she was quite happy the way things were. Who knew, though?

When someone let out an obnoxious catcall—she was guessing Vincent—she grudgingly pulled back from Kell.

His fingers just tightened on her hips. "I say we kick everyone out and see if Noel wants to babysit Reece for an hour...or two."

Biting back a smile, she shook her head. "Think again."

He grumbled good-naturedly, but she knew he would never kick any of these people out of his house. Not after they'd helped protect and save her life. Friends and family were the most important things in the world, and after these few past hellish days, Charlotte was more aware of that than ever. Now she had a brand new start with Kell and Reece and she intended to savor every moment of it.

Thank you for reading His to Protect. I really hope you enjoyed it and that you'll consider leaving a review at one of your favorite online retailers. If you don't want to miss any future releases, please feel free to join my newsletter. I only send out a newsletter for new releases or sales news. Find the signup link on my website: http://www.katiereus.com

ACKNOWLEDGMENTS

I owe a great big thank you to my readers for your continuous support, emails and reviews regarding this series! You all are amazing. I would also like to thank Carolyn Crane, Kari Walker and Laura Wright for keeping me sane. All the emails, texts and/or phone calls are so appreciated. I'm also grateful to my family for being so patient with my weird writing hours and deadlines.

A Covert Affair

Non-series Romantic Suspense
Running From the Past
Dangerous Secrets
Killer Secrets
Deadly Obsession
Danger in Paradise
His Secret Past
Retribution

Paranormal Romance
Destined Mate
Protector's Mate
A Jaguar's Kiss
Tempting the Jaguar
Enemy Mine
Heart of the Jaguar

Moon Shifter Series
Alpha Instinct
Lover's Instinct (novella)
Primal Possession
Mating Instinct
His Untamed Desire (novella)
Avenger's Heat
Hunter Reborn
Protective Instinct (novella)

Darkness Series
Darkness Awakened

Taste of Darkness
Beyond the Darkness
Hunted by Darkness
Into the Darkness

ABOUT THE AUTHOR

Katie Reus is the *New York Times* and *USA Today* bestselling author of the Red Stone Security series, the Moon Shifter series and the Deadly Ops series. She fell in love with romance at a young age thanks to books she pilfered from her mom's stash. Years later she loves reading romance almost as much as she loves writing it.

However, she didn't always know she wanted to be a writer. After changing majors many times, she finally graduated summa cum laude with a degree in psychology. Not long after that she discovered a new love. Writing. She now spends her days writing dark paranormal romance and sexy romantic suspense. For more information on Katie please visit her website: www.katiereus.com. Also find her on twitter @katiereus or visit her on facebook at: www.facebook.com/katiereusauthor.

Manufactured by Amazon.ca
Acheson, AB